Writers of the Depths

A Writers' Rooms Community Anthology

Erin Casey and Alex Penland, ed.

First edition, 2020.
The Writers' Rooms
Iowa City, IA
welcome@thewritersrooms.org

Cover art courtesy of Pixabay and Skylar Alexander Moore.

ISBN: 978-0-578-64104-1

To the writers of the community who make
The Writers' Rooms possible…thank you.

Table Of Contents

Introduction

Dear Reader, thank you for your support of The Writers' Rooms! By picking up this book, you have made your first step into joining our community as a whole.

TWR is an organization which endeavors to create a safe, inclusive community for all writers. We believe that everyone has a wealth of knowledge and a story to share. In our Rooms (which are community-led, genre-based gatherings), you bring both to the table. Each meeting consists of both discussions and time to write. Our events, which are held in conjunction with local businesses and libraries, offer a safe space in which to meet other members of your local writing community.

Our Rooms would not exist were it not for the incredible writers throughout the creative corridor. We've watched new writers learn from seasoned minds. Authors with writer's block have found a way to flourish and venture into their literary world once again. Most importantly, people have found a Room to call home, a place where they feel safe to share their voice and find help when they struggle.

The stories and poetry you're about to read are from that same community. This is our way to celebrate you and to thank everyone for helping our dream of the Rooms come to life.

Just remember, no matter where you are in your writing journey, you are never alone. You have a community waiting for you.

Best,
Erin Casey and Alex Penland, TWR Directors

Maxwell Love

Maxwell Love grew up in rural New Hampshire, graduated from Kenyon College with a degree in English, and eventually moved to Iowa by way of San Francisco. She is a co-concierge, with Nikki Herbst, of The Golden Attic. Her poetry can be found online at *Awosting Alchemy*, and elsewhere under the name Jennifer Maxwell.

Clutching the Wheel through a Storm

Maxwell Love

crisped leaves sit like frogs
asphalt under rain sings sideways
brake lights dazzle

Amelia Kibbie

Amelia Kibbie is an author, freelance writer, and secondary educator. She was born, bred, and corn-fed in the great state of Iowa, and currently resides in Iowa City. Learn more at ameliakibbie.com.

The Pearl
Amelia Kibbie

"I couldn't save him." The words tumbled from Maris' lips and over the edge of Suicide Point. She took a shuddering breath and allowed herself to look down, away from the line on the horizon where the sea met the starry sky. Her toes were inches away from the cliff's edge. Below her was a 200-foot drop into rough ocean. Jagged rocks rose up from the churning water like vicious teeth.

Maris was a skilled swimmer, and she taught survival classes on occasion. That was how she'd met Jessica—*no, don't think about her now.* Despite Maris' peak physique and her training, she knew there was no way she would survive this fall. If the rocks didn't destroy her, the current here would suck her down and rip her out to sea, so far she'd never be able to swim back.

Her breath came out of her in ragged gasps as she grappled with instinctive mortal fear. She thought of the man on the pier yesterday. A father, out for a day on the boardwalk with his wife and kids. It was so stupid. A piece of saltwater taffy down the wrong tube, and it was all over.

Saving him should have been easy enough. The wife called 911 immediately, and Maris and her fellow EMTs responded within three minutes. All they had to do was dislodge the blockage and perform CPR, which they did. When he didn't respond, they opened a trach ring. But still, the man died.

"We did everything right." Tears squeezed free from the corners of her eyes. That was the third person this week that had died unexpectedly under her care. Calls that should have been easy successes, little things in the vast world of ways of dying.

"Mar, it's just bad luck." Billy, her favorite ambulance driver, had done his best to reason with her. "This is our line of work— you can't save everyone."

But the seed had been planted, nurtured by the flood of other disasters in her life. Blake. What was she going to do about Blake? They were still married, still living together, still sleeping in the same bed, but what was broken would never be the same. Ever since he'd caught her and Jessica together, a seeping dread filled every crack of Maris' insides, slowly drowning her with the knowledge that she was going to have to get a divorce.

But how? How could she separate from him? They had just finished paying off the wedding and the honeymoon five years down the road. They shared everything—a car, a house, credit card debt. What would life be like if they had to disentangle it all? She'd have to move in with her parents, be their embarrassment. Everyone in Shell Cove would know.

Maris thought of the huge wedding portrait of her and Blake that hung above the TV in her parents' living room, framed perfection, frozen in time and happiness. She nudged herself a centimeter closer to the cliff's edge, the stones below her stark in the moonlight.

Jessica was gone. Jessica didn't care, was only disappointed that the fun was over. She had been down from the city to lifeguard at some rich guy's private beach for the summer. Jessica was twenty and beautiful and did what she wanted, and that was why Maris hadn't been able resist her.

But as soon as a nor'easter of trouble had blown up, Jessica had split, leaving Maris to deal with the aftermath.

"It's all over." Maris shuddered as she risked another look down past the toes of her sneakers. The ocean, so far below, looked black and fatal. "I have to get out. I have to get out. I can't save anyone. I just can't do it. I can't do this. I can't do this. I can't—"

Maris stepped off the cliff at Suicide Point.

***

She did not remember falling. All she knew was the impact, and the terrible pain clawing its way up her leg and arm. She was under water. Moonlight sparkled down from overhead, suddenly bright as the clouds drifted away. The rays danced, refracted from the waves above. Everything was blurry, and the salt stung her eyes, but she could just make out a pool of shadowy red spreading from her left side.

That's my blood, she thought absently. Her paramedic's mind assessed her injuries based on what she could feel, or couldn't, actually. Broken radius, broken tibia, cracked ribs, likely head trauma. And she was out of air.

I'm dying now.

The moonlight seemed to redouble its efforts. No. There was something else in the water. And it was glowing.

Maris' eyes cleared; the blurriness evaporated as though she were wearing goggles. The image before her came into focus in increments—a vaguely person-shaped figure floating on the underwater currents toward her. As it neared, Maris' heart seized in a cascade of disbelief.

The thing before her was not real. The thing in the water, swimming toward her, could not be real.

Its eyes. They were massive on the creature's elongated, oval face, glittering with mirror brightness as the moonlight rippled against them. There was a ridge below them that Maris read as a nose, but the mouth was definitely a mouth with deep purple lips that stood out against its mottled lavender flesh. It had long humanoid arms that ended in webbed-shaped hands tipped with claws. It— she—had a silhouette that suggested the ideal female hourglass, but none of the corresponding organs. Instead, the flesh of her arms, face, and shoulders gradually became the most luminescent, pearl-like scales, millions of them in perfect arrangement, each one tinier than the nail on Maris' little finger. These covered the length of her tail. A tail. Complete with undulating fins that pushed her effortlessly through the water. The only thing more breathtaking than her tail was her hair. It resembled the kinky, delicate strands that jellyfish used to catch their prey. Each tentacle seemed to have a life of its own.

She reached out for Maris, and brought their mouths together. Oxygen flooded into Maris' throat and lungs. She exhaled appreciative bubbles as a sudden thrill raced through her body. Or maybe that was the shock setting in.

In one hand, the sea creature had a strange, fleshy piece of something. Maybe it was meat, maybe it was seaweed; either way, she pressed it to Maris's face.

Maris' burning lungs opened again, and she breathed. Long, sucking breaths inflated her chest.

The tentacle-haired wonder swam around behind her and fastened the thing, whatever it was, to her head like a mask. Then, she folded Maris to herself and swam deeper, to the ocean floor. Before them was the entrance to an underwater cave. It glowed faintly, somehow, with the same uncanny luminescence that followed the creature in a shimmering trail.

Maris couldn't move her left arm, but she reached up with her other and ran her fingers over the taut flesh of the alien face. Her savior turned and smiled at her, an utterly human expression.

Maris's vision went black, and she let it come. It was peaceful.

***

The next expanse of her consciousness faded in and out, though she was sure each time she woke that time had passed.

It felt like an endless night of dreams with tendrils of darkness threading them together. The glowing cave was underwater, but she could breathe, could see perfectly. The mask remained around her face, some kind of artificial gill.

Sometimes, she would awake and be alone, anchored with seaweed to a rocky pillar. More seaweed was wrapped tightly around her arm and leg. Once, she opened her eyes to see the creature swim back into the cavern, dozens of fish wrapped in the tentacles of her hair. The creature regarded her with her mirror-like eyes and popped the silvery herring into her mouth one at a time. Behind the full purple lips were multiple rows of pointed teeth.

More often, it seemed, when she drifted back into herself, the creature was simply there, nearby, watching her with a small, encouraging smile.

She came out of her shadowy fugue, the end of the everlasting dream and the everlasting night. She was no longer tethered to the stalagmite and her body was free of the seaweed wrappings, covered only by the remains of her navy EMT uniform. The otherworldly being floated nearby and closed the distance between them with the slightest flick of her violet tail. Maris' brain struggled to process and justify what she saw. *I'm awake. I'm alive. What is she?* Her rising anxiety was suffocated by the creature's gentle touch on her arm.

The fanged mouth uttered a series of long, low tones and multi-octave clicks. Maris could not hear what the creature said; she understood that it was a language of some kind. More she felt it—it vibrated through her like the bass beat at a club but on a rainbow of frequencies. Within her came the message. She could *understand* it, somehow.

> ****Your heart was in pain*
> *So you came to sea to die*
> *Will you leave this life*
> *With so much left unfinished*
> *Like a wave*
> > *not fully formed?****

The creature took Maris around the waist and swam down to the bottom of the cavern. Maris could not believe she had never looked down to see the source of the light that filled the cave. The rocky bottom was studded with massive oysters. They lay with their mouths open wide, and in each rested a glowing gold pearl the size of a human eye.

The creature drew Maris in front of her. She reached out and touched the artificial gill on Maris' lips. Maris held her breath, and the mirror-eyed fish woman lifted the mask and gave her a long kiss. Maris could feel the teeth behind the lips. When they finally parted, the creature replaced the mask and reached down to pluck a pearl from the closest mollusk.

> ****Now you choose your path*
> *Everlasting darkened seas*
> *Or this glowing pearl*
> *Which will*
> > *return you homeward*
> *A second chance for living****

The creature held out the pearl to Maris. She moved to take it, but the creature pulled it back and spoke once more.

****For many years I swim*
My heart is a lonely moon
I am only one
There were, once, more of my kind
*So, I will mourn your leaving****

With a final melancholy note, she pressed the pearl into Maris' hand. Maris closed her fingers around it, and its glow grew so bright it blotted out all else.

***

Gulls. She could hear gulls, their calls undulating in a Doppler pattern as they swooped close to her and then wheeled away. Maris opened her eyes, and then raised her arm to shield them from the sun. A fine layer of sand sifted down onto the remains of her bra and polo. The familiar scent of popcorn and hot dogs wafted to her on the sea breeze.

She sat up in increments. Her body was stiff, but a check of her mobility revealed she had no injuries. As her eyes adjusted to the noontime sun, the pier swam into focus. The Ferris wheel spun merrily as it had every day for a hundred years, and she could hear the screams and laughter as the old wooden roller coaster thrilled its riders with twists and turns.

Maris rose to her feet and was surprised

how little effort it took. She lifted her right hand and opened it, but not without some difficulty; she'd clamped it shut so hard her finger joints were nearly frozen. There was the pearl, no longer glowing, but still incandescent with unnatural beauty.

"Hey. Hey there, are you all right?"

Maris turned and saw a cyclist in lime green spandex stopped in the bike path that ran on the other side of the grassy sand dunes.

She looked down at her ragged clothes. "I'm okay," she said, and the words made the pearl in her hand vibrate. She smiled. "I'm okay. I'm going to be okay."

It was true. When she got home to Blake, he wept in relief. She'd been gone, apparently, two days and three nights. True consideration of her death seemed to award him some kind of perspective, because as soon as they got home from the clinic (where she'd been cleared with perfect health) he took her to bed and they made love. It was good love, like in the early years.

They talked long into the night, and he accepted that she did not remember where she'd been. Finally, he absorbed her words when she apologized and said for the hundredth time that Jessica was a mistake. The chasm between them could never close, but they could build a bridge across it.

At work, people asked. She spoke openly about domestic troubles. Trying to run from them. To her surprise, people understood, and besides, EMS was short-staffed, and Maris was good at her job. In the next few weeks, she saved over twenty and lost two, and her heart allowed her to understand the significance of this ratio.

A year passed. Every night for that year, Maris fell asleep holding the pearl. Blake started talking about having kids. She decided to apply for nursing school. This was her second chance and it was beautiful.

But Maris could not forget the creature under the sea. Some days, the memories would fade, as if it had all been an elaborate, powerful dream. But the second she touched the pearl, the images roared back and crashed through her like the surf. She loved her home, her husband, her new calling, but it was a passive contentment, not a passion. And so it went, until, on the third anniversary of the day she jumped, Maris could no longer deny the call.

That day, her crew responded to a call about an elderly man wandering out on the beach. When the arrived, Maris was startled to see it was the exact same place where the cyclist had found her washed ashore.

The old man shuffled through the sand, now and then bending with some effort to pick up and examine a shell. His clothes were wet and tattered, which had prompted a passing motorist to call, but when Maris and her team approached, he smiled and waved at them. "Good morning!"

After some convincing, they coaxed him up the dunes and onto a stretcher. "I feel fine. I feel wonderful," the man told Maris as she adjusted his straps. "Everything's going to be okay."

"Hey, I think that's my line," Maris joked, but then her breath stopped. The man had something the size of a golf ball clutched in his gnarled fingers. Between his digits, she could see the opalescent surface of a massive pearl. "Did you… did you jump?" She motioned over her shoulder at the shape of Suicide Point that rose, jagged and cold, from the gently rolling sand dunes.

"I changed my mind." The man smiled at her and held the pearl to his chest.

It was real. It was all real. Maris rode to the hospital in stunned silence. The rest of the day was a confusing haze, but when night fell, she knew what she had to do.

The next day, after making her arrangements, she told Blake she had to leave.

"I don't understand." She'd expected him to be angry, to shout at her like he used to, but instead, he sank into a chair at the kitchen table and put his head in his hands. When he lifted his face, it was wet with saltwater tears. "We've been great. Haven't we?"

She agreed. It tore at her, seeing him like this. But as their life together stretched out before her, she had to turn away. Before she could speak again, he took a breath, stood, and hugged her. "I think I understand. Something's been… different since that night. That night you told me you had to go and…think. Something happened, didn't it?"

She sat down across from him and took his hands in her own. "I tried to kill myself that night."

"Oh my God."

"But I came back. I chose to live, to give this life a second chance. I know I made the right decision. I've been happy. I think we both have. But there's just… something… something I need to do yet. I can't stay."

He sniffed and nodded. "I've felt it. That you're only… partly here. Had one foot out the door, maybe." There was a long silence. "I love you," he said, "and I know you love me. I want you to do what you need to do, Maris."

"I'm going to go. There are people who… ." The last word caught in her throat, though she smiled. She'd done what she could to make sure he wouldn't be suspected of anything—written letters to her family, notified her job about her plans to move to a remote part of Nova Scotia, emptied her bank account. "You're going to be okay," she said.

He kissed her forehead and told her he loved her.

Maris drove out to the point. She picked her way through the scrubby plants and pointed rocks to the edge of the cliff. The pearl in her hand pulsed with every heartbeat. At last, she had her bare toes at the edge.

She breathed deeply to steady her heart, and found that her body was calm and ready.

Maris raised the pearl to her lips and swallowed it. Then she stepped off the cliff.

***

That night, a massive storm blew through Shell Cove, so strong it nearly toppled the historic Ferris wheel. When the clouds had cleared and the sand dried and days and nights had passed, a young man got out of his car at the base of the hill and hiked his way up to Suicide Point.

They won't stop deadnaming me. His thoughts swirled, a vortex of sorrow pulling him closer and closer to the cliff. *Just call me Seth instead of Sarah. Is that so damn hard? I can't stay there.*

But I can't move out either. I have nowhere to go. What were my choices? Transition and let everyone rip me apart? Or keep it a secret and rip myself apart? What's the point of trying? No one will ever love me.

He stood at the edge and wept. Seth's tears hit the water before he did.

I can't move my legs. I'm dying. I'm going to drown. Seth waved his arms in a pathetic attempt to surface, but it was no use.

Just as he resigned himself to the murky depths, his eyes saw what his mind would not believe. Two humanoid figures swam toward him, hand in hand. Each had a female shape, though their legs did not exist. One swam along with a powerful purple fin. The other's octopus-like tentacles undulated beneath her torso to propel her through the currents. Delicate ebony tentacles with tiny suckers descended from her scalp and swirled around her head. Her hands ended in fearsome, bony claws, but her movements were smooth and unthreatening. It seemed as though she gave him a tiny wave in greeting.

The creatures stared at him with shimmering eyes and smiled a moment before they came to his aid.

Emma Jean Meyer

Emma Jean Meyer is a Creative Writing and Economics student at Cornell College. She is the Editor-in-Chief of BOOM, Cornell's monthly literary magazine and a tutor in economics through Omicron Delta Epsilon. Her work has been featured in BOOM, Open Field, White Bear Lake Magazine, and St. Louis Park Magazine.

Maelstrom: A Full Transcription of the Soul Abandoning Ship

Emma Jean Meyer

There are many ways to die, yet two things that can be killed.

The body and the soul are connected so intimately that the death of one means death for the other. A soul needs a body to lead a human life, and a body needs a soul to drive it through this life. You are surely more familiar with the concept of bodily death which sends the soul searching for its next body. This occurs more frequently than the death of a soul, so many assume that all death is biological death.

However, after a few dozen lifetimes, a soul, too, withers away and its final body is left hollow, vacant, and useless. Souls die a little every day. Some try to live without excitement. They long to have no interruptions by the unexpected and suffer happily through monotony. These souls are hidden away for protection. They are underused and sprout cobwebs as they wait for their body to wilt, deteriorate, and die. These souls wait for one biological death after another until they are so stiff from lack of use that they reach their own ultimate end.

Loud souls burn out of overuse as they search constantly for excitement to distinguish this life from their last. They are unprotected and vulnerable to the doings of others. For both sorts, death is inevitable, and there is no in-between. Though soul death is uncommon, there is little else of intrigue it can provide, and bodily death is so familiar that it is no longer moving. So, let's consider a more interesting way in which the body and soul can be separated, a more interesting way to die.

***

Concha's life was spent at the seaside. Her lungs were callous to the effect of salt air and her toes could not remember a day spent without being dipped into the chilly water. Someone--let's say it was her father--built her a cabin on a high ocean cliff a lifetime ago so the silly little thing could indulge herself in this love affair with the sea. Alone on this cliff, she stared out her window and dreamed and thought and dreamed and thought so immensely that soon she was unable to tell the difference between her dreams and her thoughts. For several short moments in her life, she would watch two or three waves battle and thrash and, upon crowning the winner in her mind and dream-thinking about the power of waves, her soul began to wonder if it would prefer life without a body. A hairline fracture intruded the bond of Concha's body and soul. The ocean and its grey sky umbrella were the backdrop to the young girl's existence, and the catalyst in her disintegration.

She didn't believe the news when she heard that a tsunami was coming to wash away her clifftop fortress. The sea could never end her, it was her reason for living.

So, while the men and women of the nearest village packed up their things and left, Concha sat at her window and examined the shore for treasures. Conch shells were easiest to spot when they were present, but very rarely did such a creature wash up, and if one does, a beach walker must first test it with a length of driftwood to make sure that whatever was living inside was now dead and could not snip or snap when collected. On this day there were no conches, but her eyes still searched from behind a window pane.

The girl--who soon would die--surveyed the sand with her head in her hands for so long that she dozed off in the gray of the late afternoon. Less than a nighttime but more than an hour had passed her by when the screaming of waves startled Concha. The tsunami. Our dear hero had never seen blackness quite so encompassing before the flood, and never considered that such a thing was even possible in nature. The wave blocked the sky completely when it rushed toward the shore.

The village was destroyed, linens washed away, and gold looted. Heavy disappointment littered the soaking walls of the home her father may have built. Candles drowned as the horrid wave reached them one by one. She was wrong to doubt the warnings, but right that the sea would not kill her.

Life was in an instant sucked from the shore, and Concha was taken prisoner by the tsunami that had ravaged all else. Salt stung her skin and leaked into her lungs, but proved not fatal. Chill slowed her heart without stopping it, and thickened her blood without freezing it. Water cradled her, stopping the air in her body, but starving not her breathing. Now Concha sank slowly, heavily through bleak ocean.

For some time she tried to swim to the shore or to the surface, she would take whichever came more quickly. Either way, her goal was simple, don't hit the bottom. She swam straight upwards for what felt like hours before giving up and accepting that the sunlight rippling down was not getting any more intense. She swam for a long time in the direction she thought was forward before second guessing herself, worrying that she was swimming farther into the sea. She then turned around to swim an equally long time in the opposite direction. From all of this up and down and back and forth, she figured she must be within a few hundred yards of where the monster wave had placed her to begin with. Soon she gave in to the will of the currents and let her body bounce about in the depths and the dark. She gave up swimming.

Remember that hairline fracture that was earlier mentioned? Well, by now her body had been on auto pilot trying to get back to her home on the shore for so long that this fracture was now a crack. Her soul began to believe that this body would soon have to end and it would continue its journey in some new shell.

But this body was not dying. It was adapting, though it is still unclear whether the changes that followed Concha's submersion were the unconscious doings of a body clinging desperately to its soul and life or the generosity of the ocean gone awry. No, Concha's body was not dying, but her human life was now ending.

Acidic salt swirled about her, eroded her wardrobe. It licked away one thread at a time. Once taken, the thread would swim out from her body sometimes far enough that she could witness the horror of its ultimate disintegration like a poof of smoke or dirt bouncing off a hit drum. Salt stripped her, slowly at first, but with increasing speed the farther she sank. It was almost a relief to be finally bare, her coats had been suppressive and had not allowed her to witness the transformation she had fallen victim to.

As she observed now, her legs became meatier, less her and more flesh. Dumb flesh that had not been informed of what shape it was born to take on. Her thighs met each other in an intimate way and stuck together like lovers when she attempted to pull them to their sides, making her sink through the syrupy water lower than she ever imagined she could find herself.

Were her feet simply sore and pulsing or did they really have more mass than before? They didn't feel quite longer nor wider, just more. Like her thighs, her feet were attracted as if magnets of opposite polarity were embedded in her toes. It could have been the tint of the sea in her stinging eyes, but Concha was vaguely aware of her skin taking on a salty blue.

Her skin had been replaced. Her exterior no longer her, no longer hers, but some scaly fungus which had captured what once was her own flesh. Something in Concha's skin seemed to crawl slimily from scale to scale, but her eyes could never quite catch it. The only glimmer of her old body that remained was the pale white color some of the scales possessed.

Concha reached down to where her knees had once been, the two hinges of her limp legs had melded into one mighty joint. Her stomach lurched on the sight of the mucus clinging to her body from the naval down.

No matter how much the girl exerted herself, she could no longer pull apart her thighs and her feet were indistinguishable from one another. She had become a torso resting atop a massive limb.

Sinews emerged from crevices she couldn't relate to any human anatomy, and little bony structures billowed in the water's current, threatening to snap off at any moment. Would it hurt if they did? She didn't want to find out.

Though Concha had no way of knowing, her pupils had been bleached by the dark of the water. Or, rather, a light had developed behind her pupils to illuminate the bleakness she faced and allowed her to interpret the world around her in a way she couldn't with human eyes. This light gave the illusion of eyes blank and white.

Concha's human life was over. Something of her soul sensed this and began the process of moving on. But, it must be repeated that this body, though no longer human, was healthy. In fact, this body was brand new and thus repaired the crack that had formed between Concha's old body and her soul. There was no reason for her soul to flee, but it had not felt the change, only witnessed those things that should have killed her and the following adaptation which her soul mistook as a body rotting. It could not escape when it tried desperately now to find its new body for this was its new body.

Concha's soul beat at her, trying to abandon ship, but it was trapped. This soul believed that its body was dead and that it must separate from this body to survive. So her soul did the unthinkable, it severed this renewed connection to its body, sealing Concha's fate.

The body and soul were now independent of one another, yet the soul could still not escape this healthy body. It could not move on to another shell in time and so it withered, as all souls do. The body went limp and was bullied about by the waves which had before fostered it. Concha, this name we have given to the connection between this particular pair of body and soul, was dead. Her soul became sea foam, and her body washed up days later on the shore below the home on the cliff that may have been built by her father.

Concha was an unrecognizable shell and the only case of this rarest of deaths. Waves lapped against her sinewy limbs, sand stuck to her white eyes, and the foamy remains of her soul collected at her hips where the water and earth collided.

Since the tsunami, the villagers had returned to their homes, concluded that the girl on the cliff was never coming back, and began to sort through her things to see what could be of use to them in their reparations. A small child from the group of scavengers was fiddling with the lone shard of glass that had stuck to Concha's window frame. The rascal peaked down to the shore in the hopes of finding a conch to give to his mother, but instead discovered a monster. A moment later, he was skipping from outcropping to outcropping to reach the sand. Once close enough to hop onto the beach, he released his grip on the cliffside and tugged a stick free from a whole tree that had washed up. He poked Concha.

But there was nothing inside.

Linda Muller

Linda Muller's work can be found in the University of Iowa Writing Center's "Voices," and in 2018 "Lyrical Iowa." When she isn't arguing with her husband about which one of them the dog loves the most, she can be found in coffee shops, reading, writing, or procrastinating.

Into the Past
Linda Muller

"So we beat on, boats against the current, borne back ceaselessly into the past."
– F. Scott Fitzgerald, The Great Gatsby

Imagine turning ages
Into the hours passing
behind mirrors
of the heart
of the past.
Broken

Decades graduate into offertorial smoke obscuring the banks
of time. Photos taken to prove that life was in your hand,
in that hollow cigarette of memory that burns
against the grain of each picture.

My eyes believe each tear that you see smoldering the fire.
Every tear that protects you (us)
transforms past strangers
into uncles and lawyers.

Floating in photo boats, in dream travels across the back
of the sky, wondering if it always looks like the back
of a mirror – Letters arrive in my hand
and the current shifts into the past.

Ross T. Byers

Ross T. Byers lives beneath your bed and feeds on your nightmares. He is also one of the concierges of The Parchment Lounge.

For your safety, do not follow him on Twitter @RTByers or visit his website rosstbyers.com.

The Horror at the Beach

Ross T. Byers

Amy didn't know when killing monsters started feeling dull and quotidian, but she knew she hated it. Take this night, for instance. There were rumors, if you knew where to ask, of some sort of hideous monster terrorizing the beach, so she and her partner in violence, Sigurd, were on their way to slay it. She should have been excited about the prospect, but she would rather have been out dancing. She stared down at her scarred left palm as they approached the shore. Sigurd eased the car into the parking spot adjacent to the boardwalk. There were no other vehicles around. They got out, Sigurd retrieving the harpoon he'd hidden beneath a tarp on the back seat.

"You want anything for this?" he asked. "I've got a lot of goodies in my trunk."

"No, I'll be fine," said Amy.

They walked across the narrow boardwalk and down to the beach, which was very dark. The sand gave off a sickly gleam, but the water was a blank onyx expanse given only the vaguest definition wherever the light from the waxing moon limned the surf. It was an unusually clear sky, and Amy could see several stars shining through the light pollution. Or maybe they were just satellites in low orbit.

The beach was deserted, and it wasn't just the dark keeping people away. The tide had an overpowering chemical stench. No one in the city ever came down to the beach unless they wanted to dispose of something. If people ever got the craving for some fun in the sun they went somewhere else, like up to Jersey or down to Florida.

Of course, there were also those rumors of something monstrous lurking offshore.

About a dozen feet north of Amy and Sigurd a large outflow pipe jutted out of a hill and pumped a steady flow of yellow sludge into the ocean. There was no chain link fence keeping people away, or even signs posted warning people about the dangers of industrial waste. She figured that was probably another reason no one came to this beach.

"This looks like the place," said Amy. "Would you lay odds on this thing having tentacles? I'm pretty sure it's going to have tentacles. I mean, judging by the course my life has taken recently, you know, with that idiot sorcerer and his 'nameless horror', then that thing in the subway tunnels, of course the sea monster's going to have tentacles. I hate tentacles."

Sigurd shrugged. "Yeah, well, life sucks."

"I'm glad you're in a good mood."

"Look, it might not have tentacles. Maybe it's a shark-human hybrid, or a lobster man, or something stupid like that. Maybe it's just a good old-fashioned sea serpent."

Amy sighed wistfully. "Wouldn't that be nice."

Sigurd stuck his harpoon in the sand and began to strip.

"Here's the plan," he said. "I'm going to swim out there and then either lure or drive it ashore. Once it's on the beach, you do your thing and kill it."

"Solid. Are you going to fight it naked?"

"I don't own a wetsuit."

"Would you at least keep your pants on?" Sigurd's jeans dropped to the sand. "Too heavy. Make sure no one steals those, alright? My wallet's in there."

"There's no one here," Amy said to his back as he walked naked towards the sea, harpoon in hand and KA-BAR between his teeth. "If there was someone here, they would have called the cops because this isn't a nude beach."

Sigurd strode confidently into the surf, head high and shoulders back, but he paused as the lapping waves reached his knees.

"Is something wrong?" Amy asked.

He took the knife from his mouth with his free hand, then craned his head back and said, "This water feels disgusting."

"You did the see the industrial waste drainage pipe just over there, right?"

"I guess that explains why it tingles. You probably don't want to swim in this."

"Having second thoughts?"

"No," said Sigurd, taking a step forward.

He whipped out of the water thirty feet into the air, dangling upside-down from a tentacle wrapped around his ankle. It shook him screaming back-and-forth. At least a dozen more tentacles exploded out of the water, a forest of waving limbs all tugging and battering at him. The harpoon sailed out of the night sky and skewered the beach near Amy's feet.

"Crap," she said. "I knew there would be tentacles."

The monster smashed Sigurd repeatedly against the beach, raising a cloud of sand. He was still screaming, so at least he was still conscious. Amy plucked the harpoon from the beach. She traced the tentacles until she found their nexus beneath the waves, a slight hump in the water briefly outlined by the moon, then reared back and hurled the harpoon. It glittered in the moonlight as it sliced through the air and thunked down into the hump.

Bulls-eye.

Water sprayed everywhere as the creature thrashed. It lost its grip on Sigurd, flinging him screaming into the sky before he fell screaming onto the beach. He landed in a crumpled ball with the crunch of many broken bones.

"Gotta say, I'm really loving your plan."

Sigurd coughed, a puff of sand rising from his bloodied lips. His body was already twisting back into its original shape. He let out a pained moan and said, "I got sand in my eyes."

The monster surfaced, roaring its displeasure. The tentacles formed a ring around its hooked beak, the harpoon embedded in the flesh between dangling like a toothpick. Clusters of eyes, glowing with a weak green phosphorescence, were set into the side of its cigar-shaped body. More eyes rose on stalks along its back. It stood up on eight thick insectile legs, water streaming off its carapace, and approached the beach. The ground shuddered with each ponderous step it took.

"Great," said Amy. "Please tell me you have more harpoons."

"Trunk."

"Keys?"

"Pants."

Amy ran to the discarded jeans and knelt down. A tentacle whipped over her head and slammed the beach behind her, the wind from its passing tugging at her short hair. She dug out the car keys and turned to jingle them at Sigurd, who had risen to a sitting position. He'd managed to stab himself with his own knife when he landed. He pulled it out of his side.

"I'll keep it distracted," he said.

"You do that," said Amy, sprinting towards the car.

The sand made running difficult, slowed her a bit, but she still reached the car in less than a minute. Amy thrust the key at the trunk lock but missed, putting a long scratch in the paint beside the keyhole. She hissed and flashed back to some of the hits she'd taken when she first started sparring with Sigurd. She took a breath, then fit the key in and threw open the trunk. She blinked at the arsenal stored within. There was a broadsword and a fire ax, several kinds of handguns, a sawn-off pump-action shotgun, and some sort of submachine gun, the kind she'd only seen in movies before. Pushed all the way in the back, however, was a crossbow with an attached quiver. Amy grabbed it and, after a moment of thought, took the fire ax as well.

She turned around and saw Sigurd standing on the beach, staring down the approaching leviathan and hollering a war cry, the ichor-slathered knife in one hand and a severed bit of tentacle in the other. The monster bellowed back at him, and the severed tentacle in Sigurd's fist lashed out and wrapped around his throat. His shout choked off and he sawed at the outstretched bit of tentacle with his knife. When she reached him, he had cut through the tentacle and it writhed in the sand at his feet. He stomped on it, grinding it into the beach with his heel. Amy tossed the ax over and he caught it out of the air.

"Why'd you bring me this?"

"I thought it might be useful for, you know, chopping tentacles."

"Why didn't you bring me the UMP?"

"I don't know what that is."

It's the sub-"

A thick tentacle, balled up at the end like the head of a mace, smashed into Sigurd from above, crushing him into the sand. Amy rolled her eyes and turned to face the approaching monstrosity. It fixed its many-eyed stare on her and splayed out its tentacles in a threat display, bellowing. She really hated the part that came next, but there wasn't any choice. There never was.

Gripping the crossbow, she sliced her left hand open on the sharp edge of the quarrel. She clenched her fist and dribbled blood onto the broadhead and smeared more on the shaft for good measure. She rested the crossbow on her forearm, sighted the monster, and fired. The bloody bolt cut through the night and hit home. The beast reared back and howled at the sky, flailing about. Amy narrowly avoided getting crushed by jumping and rolling as a tentacle plowed into the beach, spraying up sand.

Sigurd coughed and spluttered from the crater he was lying in and said, "-machine gun."

She hadn't brought him a gun because they were noisy and would bring them unwanted attention. People were weird; they wouldn't report the monster out of fear of being thought of as crazy, but they would absolutely report any gunfire they heard. Then the police would show up and it would cause a whole scene and, really, it was just better for everyone if that never happened.

The creature was occupied with trying to pull out the bolt, its tentacles too large for the job, so Amy ran over to Sigurd.

"Can you move?"

"Gonna be a few minutes. You kill the thing?"

"Yeah, it should die any second now."

The beast bellowed out a cry full of rage and pain, loud enough to make Amy wince and cover her ears.

"Yep," she said. "Any second now."

The creature lumbered towards the beach, huge gouts of water spraying up with each step, the ground shaking at its approach.

"Crap," said Amy, reloading the crossbow.

"Didn't you get your blood into it?"

"Yes."

"Then shouldn't it be dead?"

"Also yes."

"It's big; maybe it needs more."

"It only ever takes a little."

"Bleed on that quarrel."

"I am bleeding."

"Bleed faster."

"Not helping!"

The monster was almost on top of them, its beak open wide to swallow them down. It's breath gusted over them, making Amy's jacket billow and flap. It stank of rotting seaweed and dead fish. Amy raised the crossbow and fired another blood-smeared bolt, which sank deep into the monster's flesh. It scuttled backwards, roaring in agony. Its eyeballs exploded, one after another, blue flame erupting from the sockets and stalks. It flailed its tentacles blindly. More blue fire streamed from its gaping beak. The beast stumbled, burning and screaming. Then it imploded, crumpling into itself until nothing but a handful of glowing embers and ashes remained, which drifted away on the gentle night breeze.

"There," said Amy. "See? Dead."

"Yay," said Sigurd, then coughed, spat blood, and moaned. "I think I can taste my spleen."

"Of course you'd know what a spleen tastes like."

"You laugh, but the healing is just as painful as the wounding."

She held her left hand palm-up, watching the blood pool. It looked black in the moonlight.

He said, "There's a first-aid kit in the glove box. Why don't you go patch yourself up? I'm just going to rest here for a minute."

"I'm going," said Amy, trudging back towards the car. "Make sure to put your pants back on before you come up."

She'd left the keys in the trunk lock, so she retrieved them. She let herself in on the passenger side and opened the glove box. The first-aid kit was clearly a recent addition. It rested beside a stubby revolver and a large knife. Sigurd, being immortal, had no need of it. He'd bought it for her sake. Or maybe it was for the adolescent daughter he'd recently adopted. Maybe both of them. Amy couldn't imagine him allowing anyone else in his car.

She pulled out the first-aid kit, revealing a quarter-empty bottle of rye whiskey. After staring at it for a moment she grabbed it too. She pulled the cork out with her teeth, spat it into the driver's seat, and took a slug. It burned down to her belly and spread its comforting warmth. It would help with what came next.

She set the whiskey between her feet, then mopped the blood away from her palm with a bit of gauze. She opened a bottle of isopropyl alcohol and poured it over the long, shallow cut. She clenched her teeth and hissed as pain lanced up her arm. She slapped a large bandage over the cut and wrapped it up with more gauze.

Leaning her head back against the headrest, Amy breathed out a sigh, trying to ignore the pain throbbing up from her hand. Sigurd complained sometimes, but his body recovered from any wound. It was miraculous. She had to do things the old fashioned way, with bandages and sutures.

Then again, he was basically just her meat shield. She was the one who actually got the job done, spilling her blood all over the city to kill and ward away monsters.

She craned her head back to look out at the few visible stars, then down at her bandaged, aching hand. The sea beast had provided a brief thrill, but now it was gone. She pondered how her life had wound up so far from where she used to imagine it being. The crunch of sand alerted Amy to Sigurd's approach. He was back in his clothes, but his face was streaked with blood and ichor and he limped while he walked. He settled into the driver's seat.

"I'm starving," he said. "Want some sushi? My treat."

"Nah, I've gotta work tomorrow. I should get to bed."

"Alright," he said, and fired up the engine.

They drove off, leaving the quiet beach behind. Amy leaned her head against the window and entertained a brief fantasy about going to a university to study dance, meeting new people, and having a different life. Then she let it evaporate. She knew she was stuck slaying monsters. It was in her blood.

Ellen Rozek

Ellen Rozek is a young adult and new adult writer who loves experimenting with different genres. Her nonfiction work has appeared on the Disability in KidLit and National Novel Writing Month blogs, as well as on The Financial Diet website. When she's not telling stories, she's probably reading them.

Out of Reach

Ellen Rozek

The day Harlan Jones made the biggest mistake of his life was perfect in every way: blue skies, calm seas, and a fair wind that filled the Enchantment's sails, propelling her toward home. It was weather for keeping watch or sunning on deck, not checking the cargo that filled the ship's hold to ensure nothing had been tampered with. But Jones had a job to do, so he reluctantly headed below. After months of lean rations and low pay, even the most loyal crew members could be tempted to pocket a bit of this or that to sell at the end of the voyage.

As he neared the ship's stern he heard a soft sound like the sudden intake of a breath followed by an unmistakable sneeze. Jones reached for the revolver he always wore at his belt, scanning the hold for any sign of another person as he slid the gun free. The cluster of barrels anchored between the low ceiling and the wall were exactly as they should be, and it wasn't until he turned to search elsewhere that a thought occurred to him. Though the barrels' sloping sides left no room for anyone but a half-starved urchin to squeeze through, it might still be possible for a stubborn stowaway or a sticky-fingered sailor to clamber over the top and conceal himself in the space between all of them.

Adjusting his grip on his revolver, Jones readied himself, lunged back toward the barrels, and shoved the nearest one just far enough to the left to look into that center space.

From out of the shadows, someone looked back. Jones jerked away, leveling the revolver at the space between the stranger's eyes. "C'mon, then," he said. "Out where I can see you, and no funny business."

The stowaway said nothing, but it wasn't until the top of their head crested the barrels that Jones understood why. Bedraggled, blonde hair hung limply on both sides of an unmistakably female face. And when she squeezed through the space he'd created, her damp blue dress clung to a figure that was unmistakably female as well.

Somehow Jones kept his grip on his revolver, but his jaw plummeted straight toward the floor. "How in the—?" he started to say, then stopped. Stowaway or not, this was still a lady. "How did you manage to slip aboard?" he asked instead.

"All talk about the nature of sailors aside," she said, bracing herself against the nearest barrel, "your night watch was remarkably unobservant."

Jones bit back an additional curse. He'd have to talk with the crew about that later. "Who are you?"

A muscle in her jaw tightened. "I don't suppose there's much point in telling you my name if you're only going to throw me overboard," she said, brushing her hair out of her face with one filthy hand. Her eyes were as green as the rolling fields outside the village he'd left behind, and Jones lost a few too many seconds staring into them before he was able to respond.

"Stowaways are locked in the brig," he said gruffly, "not fed to the sharks." Although the brig wouldn't be any safer once the rest of the crew discovered they had a woman in their midst. "What are you even doing here?"

"Trying to get back to England," the stowaway said, and in spite of how hoarse her voice was there was no mistaking her accent.

"In the hold of a merchant's vessel?"

"I had few other options. My father's gambling ruined my family's financial security, and the deal he made in his latest reckless attempt to dig us out of debt got himself, my mother, and my sister killed. There wasn't money left for passage home."

Then how did you survive? Jones wanted to ask, but thought better of it. To have made it this far took as much survival instinct as stubbornness—qualities she clearly had in spades. "Where did you board?"

"Calcutta."

"That was ten days ago," Jones said, holstering his revolver. He could overpower her with his own two hands if he had to, as ragged as she was. *How the hell had nobody noticed her?* "When's the last time you've eaten?"

"My provisions ran out three days ago," she said. "I'd found the water drums below decks, but no food."

No wonder she looked so unsteady and sounded so rough. At least the captain would order her fed if he turned her in. "What's left for you in England?" Jones asked, weighing his options.

"I have aunts and uncles there who might take me in. If not, I can learn a trade or join a convent."

"A woman like you has no place in a convent."

For the first time since he'd found her she looked away from him, her gaze landing on the Enchantment's sloping side as though she could see through it to the future beyond. "Better a convent than the street," she said quietly.

Jones clenched his jaw, his hands. *Better to turn her in*, he thought, but his feet refused to move. Maybe it was because she'd stolen nothing besides a few sips of water, or because she still conducted herself like a lady, unpleasant circumstances or no. But when she met his eyes again Jones was forced to admit—if only to himself—that his reasons for wanting to help her were much less sensible.

"Are you opposed to hard work?"

Relief flashed across her face, there and gone before he could blink. "Not at all."

"Good." He removed the flask from his hip and offered it to her, impressed when she swallowed without choking or wincing. "Then you're going to stay here while I find you something else to wear. And after that we're going to cut your hair."

*
**

It took the sailor less time than Nadia would've expected to return, bearing an armful of clothes for her. "You can change back there," he said, thrusting them into her hands and nodding at the cluster of barrels. "The crew will be expecting us both on deck soon, and you'll need to look the part. Otherwise they'll sniff you out right away."

"And if they do?" Nadia asked, half-hoping he had a plan of some sort. The flat, hard look he gave her instead was far less reassuring.

"You'd best hope they don't."

Nadia tightened her grip on the bundle of borrowed clothes. No need to ask him what might happen if she was incapable of fooling the other sailors. She could fill in the gaps for herself.

"I'll give you some privacy," the sailor said, turning away from her.

"I need help with my dress first," she blurted out, and he stopped dead in his tracks. Her heart pounded so loudly that she was certain he could hear it, but she made herself meet his gaze when he faced her again. "That wasn't an invitation," she added, and the sailor's lips quirked upwards.

"Understood," he responded. "Turn around."

Folding her arms across her chest, Nadia did as he asked. If he decided to get her out of her skirts altogether she'd have no way to stop him, especially without access to a weapon. But the sailor loosened the ties on her dress, the lacing on her corset, and her stays without making any effort to touch her. He'd clearly had plenty of practice with women's clothing, Nadia recognized that much, but he also let her be as soon as he'd finished. "I'll keep watch by the stairs," he said. "Come and find me once you're dressed."

The borrowed trousers were a bit long and the borrowed shirt far too big, but the extra material helped Nadia conceal her figure, along with the cloth he'd provided for her to bind her chest. They were also blessedly dry, which was more than she could say for the dress. "Better," the sailor grunted when she reappeared. "Now your hair."

He produced a pair of scissors from one of the many pouches attached to his belt and beckoned her closer. "It's not going to look pretty," he said, taking a lock in his hand. "Not like it is now."

"That's probably for the best," Nadia said. Pretty was all well and good on land, but it wasn't enough to keep her safe at sea.

When he'd finished, the ends stopped just above her ears—too short to hang in her face or stick to the back of her neck. Nadia felt instantly lighter. "How does it look?" she asked.

"Not ugly enough to be a man," he said, stashing the scissors away. "But as long as you play your part, it should be enough. Your voice is too female to hide, so it's best you don't speak at all. If you stick close to me, the rest of the crew might give you less trouble for playing the mute."

"Once this conversation is over, I'll be the quietest person you've ever met."

"You'd better be," he said. "Your return home depends on it."

Nadia swallowed her retort. Antagonizing the man who had agreed to keep her identity a secret wouldn't be wise. "I appreciate your help," she said, "and I assure you that I won't do anything to jeopardize my safety or your standing, Mr. . . . ."

"Jones," the sailor said, like he wasn't sure if she was mocking him or not. When Nadia kept quiet, he gestured up the stairs with a quick lift of his chin. "I'm going to go up on deck and speak to the captain. I want you to follow me in a few minutes, after I've come up with some excuse."

Nadia's shoulders stiffened. Convincing the captain that she belonged on the ship would be a much more difficult task than convincing the crew. "Will he listen to you?"

"I'm his second mate," Jones said matter-of-factly. "He should."

***

In the interest of protecting himself and the stowaway, Jones kept his story simple. He'd explained to the captain that they'd picked up a new crewman at last port—a young English sailor willing to work in exchange for free passage home. And when the captain had asked why the matter had never been brought to his attention, Jones told him the sailor was mute.

"Mute?" the captain repeated. He was a fair man, but Jones knew he was considering the problems a mute sailor might present.

"Yes, sir," Jones said. "He's a hard worker, and he's been doing the duties expected of him. Can write clear enough too, when it comes to that."

The captain frowned, considering. "And he's English?"

"That's what he said."

The silence stretched between them, broken only by the slap of waves against the hull drifting in through the open window. "You know I trust your judgment, Jones," the captain said at last. "But in the future I expect an introduction before you bring a new sailor aboard."

"Understood," Jones said, bowing his head. "My apologies, captain."

"Where is he?" the captain asked, rising from his seat.

"The main deck," Jones said, praying the lady had done what he'd asked. "Let me take you to him."

He spotted her the instant they exited the captain's quarters, standing with her back to them both as she looked out over the starboard railing. *It's a good thing she's thin*, Jones thought, his gaze drifting down over the subtle curves of her ass. Even in a pair of borrowed men's clothes, her hair cut short, he still couldn't see her as anything other than a woman.

"What's his name?" the captain asked, drawing Jones's attention away from the stowaway. Squinting against the sunlight, he studied her just intently enough to make Jones squirm.

"Gary," Jones said, choosing the first name that came to mind.

"Gary," the captain repeated, as though testing it for its accuracy. Then, in a louder voice, he called, "Gary, come here."

The lady turned, caught Jones's eye, and made her way toward them. Jones made the introductions, cringing inside when the two of them shook hands, but the captain made no comment on either the strength of her grip or the feel of her skin.

"You've sailed before, Gary?" he asked.

The stowaway nodded.

"How many voyages?'

She held up three fingers.

The captain glanced over at Jones, his eyes curious and hard in equal measure. Jones held his gaze. In this game of chance, the most important thing he could do was bluff convincingly.

"Cook might need some assistance, if you want to start him there," the captain said at last. "I'll leave it to you to determine where he'll fall into the night watch rotation."

"Yes, sir," Jones said, beckoning 'Gary' forward. The sooner he could get her away from the captain, the better he'd feel. "I'll explain things while I get his bunk moved."

Only after they were out of earshot did Jones let out his breath in a rush. "You've got Lady Luck on your side, miss," he muttered as they descended the stairs to the crews' quarters. Hopefully, that was where she would stay for the remainder of the voyage.

*****

Within three weeks, Nadia could barely remember why she'd been so eager to masquerade as a crew member. Her muscles ached from overuse, and her hands were stiff and rough with blisters. To make matters worse, Jones had done nothing but snap at her about the quality of her work ever since he'd helped her hide. When he'd agreed to keep her secret, she'd assumed that he'd be looking out for her. Now, she wondered if he wanted to convince her to give herself up. Only Nadia's stubbornness kept her from fulfilling his wishes; only her pride kept her from tears.

She was swabbing the floors on the mess deck when Jones appeared in the doorway. Nadia glanced his way, acknowledging him, but kept working. He'd likely come to yell at her about something anyway; she wasn't going to give him a reason to call her lazy as well.

But all Jones said was, "We're dropping anchor to swim, if you're interested."

Nadia glanced up at him with wide eyes, shaking her head hard. *What was he thinking?*

"You don't have to," Jones went on. "But it'll look strange if you don't."

And looking strange might mean the difference between being discovered and going unnoticed. Nadia bit her lip, considering.

"Put on a colored shirt and jump in with clothes on," Jones said. "You won't stand out that way, I promise. And besides," he added, his voice becoming almost friendly, "it's still warm enough that you won't get cold. Finish up here and then dump the bucket. You can change while the others are on deck."

It was an order, however well-meaning, so Nadia got to her feet and headed below. Keeping an eye on the stairs, she ducked into her bunk and changed as quickly as she could. She'd just finished lacing her shirt when thunderous footsteps announced the bo'sun's arrival.

"What are you doing down here?" he asked, spotting her immediately.

Nadia ducked her head, avoiding his gaze as she placed her sweaty work shirt to the side. It had taken her less than three days to determine that she should avoid the bo'sun at all costs. The other sailors teased her without malice, but the bo'sun tormented her with a cruelty that made Jones's criticisms seem kind.

"Can't answer me?" the bo'sun continued. "Or not going to?"

Nadia's blood ran cold. *Had he guessed? Or did he know?*

The bo'sun smirked in response to her silence, taking a short step toward her. Another. Nadia's hands curled into fists, her breath coming faster as she searched for an escape.

"You get lost down there, Gary?" Jones called from above, and Nadia seized what might be her only opportunity, darting past the bo'sun's burly body and up the stairs. Jones was waiting nearby, and his eyes darkened at the fear still in hers. "Are you all right?" he asked in a much lower voice, and Nadia made herself nod.

I'm fine, she mouthed, and it was almost the truth. When he treated her like an equal instead of a nuisance, she was fine with him beside her.

"Come on, Jones!" bellowed one of the other sailors, his head and shoulders bobbing in the bright blue waves. "Get your arse in the water."

"What about the rest of me?" Jones bellowed back, but he actually smiled as he stripped off his shirt. Nadia stared at him, unsure if his smile or the muscles in his shoulders and back, flexing beneath sun-browned skin captivated her more. He performed a neat dive into the water, and the empty space on the deck where he'd stood made it easier to think clearly.

Come on, now, she thought. *You know better.* Then she gave her shirt a quick tug, just to make sure the ties would hold, and leapt in after him.

After the heat of the past few days, the cool water was more refreshing than Nadia could have imagined. She broke the surface with one powerful kick, treading water for a moment until she regained her air supply before diving back under again and coming up a short distance away from the rest of the crew. There, she rolled onto her back and spread out her arms so she could float. As the seawater flowed into and out of her ears, the crew's splashing and shouting faded away. She drifted peacefully, the sun warm on her face, until a nearby splash startled her upright.

"Sorry," Jones said, his gruff voice drifting toward her. "Didn't mean to scare you." He treaded water just out of arm's reach, his presence putting her more at ease and making her more self-conscious all at once. The heat in his gaze was palpable, and it made Nadia shiver for reasons that had nothing to do with the ocean's chill.

***

Once, Jones had retreated to the poop deck when he needed to think. But ever since 'Gary' had come aboard, he'd wound up watching her instead. Even though she'd become a competent crew member, accepted and well-liked in spite of her silence, he still worried that someone might discover her secret. It was one thing for him to know there was a woman on board. He could keep his hands to himself, no matter how hard it was. (And when she'd climbed out of the sea, her clothes plastered to her body, her lips red and moist, it had been damn hard indeed.) The other sailors might not.

Jones folded his arms across his chest, forcing himself to gaze out to sea instead of at the deck. Treating her like any other crew member was the best protection he could offer, even if the space between them felt less bearable with every passing week. He'd told himself dozens of times that he couldn't really know her, that they'd only spoken once. But he still couldn't deny that he'd spent three sleepless nights trying to shake the image of her peacefully floating from his mind, or that he remembered every single time he'd made her smile, or that not knowing her name was slowly driving him mad.

Less than a week later, Jones was grabbing a needle and thread from his bunk to mend the hole in his trousers when he heard voices on the stairs.

"Awfully pretty for a boy, you are."

Jones's hands went cold despite the warm air. He abandoned his search and headed straight for the stairs, where he found the bo'sun backing her up against the wall, clutching both of her wrists in one meaty hand. "Let's see where it comes from."

"That's enough," Jones said, stepping around the corner and up onto the landing.

The bo'sun looked over at him. "*Boy's* hiding something," he said.

"He's mute," Jones said. "He's likely hiding a few things." The rage pounding through him made it difficult to keep his voice steady. "Let him go."

But the bo'sun gave him a wicked grin, twisting her wrists above her head and making a grab for her chest with his free hand. She arched away from him and Jones lunged forward, driving his shoulder into the man's ribs. The bo'sun stumbled backwards, grabbing the railing to steady himself, and

Jones took the opportunity to deliver a punch that snapped his head backwards as he forced himself between them. "That was an order," Jones snarled, his breath coming hard in his chest. "Stand down."

Blood streaming from his nose, the bo'sun turned on his heel with a wordless snarl and stormed back up the stairs. The woman beside him was white with fear, but Jones didn't dare reach out to her no matter how much he wanted to. "C'mon," he said instead, determined to keep her by his side for a few moments more. "Follow me."

He led her back to his bunk for lack of any better ideas, scanning the bunks around it to make sure they were deserted. "Are you all right?" he asked, once he knew they were alone.

She—he couldn't think of her as 'Gary' just then—nodded, but her trembling gave her away. He'd never seen her that frightened, and it tore at him. "Are you sure?"

This time she shook her head, tears flowing faster than she could dash them away. Without thinking, Jones reached out and put a hand on her back. The woman leaned into his body as though that was all the encouragement she needed, her head coming to rest on his shoulder.

Not good, Jones thought, even as he wrapped both arms around her and settled his chin against the crown of her head. She fit perfectly against him, and the press of her hips against his hips, her chest against his chest made him dizzy. *Not good at all.*

***

Jones had barely acknowledged her since their encounter with the bo'sun, and Nadia couldn't stand it. She still felt him watching her sometimes, but his attention was always elsewhere whenever she dared glance his way. She'd considered making some sort of mistake at her work just to get him to approach her, only to reject the possibility because of how desperate it felt. No matter how lonely she was, or how badly she wanted to know what he felt for her, she still couldn't risk talking to him. Not when the bo'sun had already set his sights on her.

After several long, exhausting days of trying to watch her own back, she was jumpier than usual during her turn at night watch. Low-hanging clouds masked the moon and darkened the skies, and a stiff breeze made the sails rustle and groan. Nadia had kept half an eye on the horizon and half an eye on the stairs for hours, straining to listen for footsteps over the ambient sounds of the sea.

She'd just completed another circuit of the poop deck when a man's head and shoulders crested the stairs. She leapt backwards, legs nearly buckling when she realized it was just Jones. He held up his hands, a silent indicator that he meant no harm, but Nadia glared at him anyway, clutching her heart to convey a silent message of her own. *You scared me.*

"I'm sorry," he said, coming to join her at the railing.

Nadia folded her arms across her chest, feeling, as always, the bindings that kept her breasts hidden. If she'd been able to speak, she would've asked him why he'd been so determined to pretend that she didn't exist.

Having him avoid her had been a torment worse than those days huddled between the barrels, watching her freshwater supply dwindle to nothing. This man, this sailor, was her anchor, the only person who knew her true identity. For that, and for reasons she was just beginning to understand, she wanted him close.

Jones was speaking again, but it took her a moment to hear the words. "—couldn't sleep without making sure you were safe."

He glanced over at her, searching her face for a response the way he had so many times in the past. He'd become all too good at reading her, but Nadia knew he might never guess how she felt unless she showed him.

She'd half-expected her hands to shake, once she finally got the chance to touch him, but they were steady as could be when she laid one against his cheek. Close as they were she could hear Jones's breath catch, his eyes darken with some unknown emotion as he stared into hers. She had no idea what he was searching for this time, but when he kissed her she knew that he'd found it.

The world seemed to stop as his lips melded against hers, his arms coming around her to hold her against him. Nadia leaned into the solidness of his body, letting him support them both as she tangled her fingers in his hair. How long they stood there, too lost in each other to bother with anything else, she had no idea.

When they finally paused for breath, Jones leaned back just far enough for their noses to touch. "What's your name?" he asked, as though it was a matter of great significance. "Your real name?"

Nadia dragged her fingers over his cheek and down the side of his neck, delighting in the way that he shivered. "Nadia," she said. "What's yours?"

His answering smile warmed her straight through. "Harlan."

"Harlan Jones." Nadia tested the name, the way it felt on her lips. "I like it."

"Not as pretty as Nadia," Jones said, before claiming her mouth with his once more.

***

The next morning came all too quickly, but for the chance to hear Nadia's voice and kiss her lips, Jones knew he would've happily stayed up all night.

His thoughts were so full of her that he didn't realize something was wrong until he reached the main deck, where the crew stood in straight lines facing the captain and first mate, with Nadia between them. Her gaze went straight to him, but Jones couldn't meet it. Not when there was still a chance that his reputation might protect them both.

"It was recently brought to my attention," the captain began, as Jones took his place in line, "that this young man—" he rested a hand on Nadia's shoulder, "—is lying about both his muteness . . . and something else as well." The captain let his hand fall and stepped forward, turning sharply to face Jones. "You brought him on board, Jones," he said. "What do you have to say for yourself?"

"If there are lies, I haven't heard them," Jones said shortly, sticking to the facts as he knew them. "The lad's been a good worker.

I'm not concerned with his reasons for speaking or not."

The captain didn't blink. "Then you won't mind if I take a closer look at the situation," he said, drawing a knife from his belt. In one swift motion, he seized Nadia's wrist and sliced open her shirt, ripping it away from her body.

She cried out, curling her arms around herself in an attempt to hide the binding covering her chest, and Jones leapt forward with a shout. He realized instantly what he'd done, what the captain had forced him to do, and he froze.

"You see, Jones," the captain continued. "I don't think our young miss here is the only one who's been lying."

Jones didn't speak. He couldn't. Anything he could have said would've only made their situation worse.

"Tie her to the railing," the captain said, looking over the crew. "And if the bo'sun would fetch the cat o' nine tails?"

The bo'sun cast a devilish smirk at Jones before hustling below decks. A few others dragged Nadia to the railing, her long-stifled voice pouring forth in a torrent of soft pleas— *let me explain, this was my doing, if I could speak to the captain myself*—while the remaining men surrounded Jones. Some avoided his gaze when he tried to make eye contact, while others simply glared at him.

"Shirt off, Jones," the captain said, taking a few steps forward. "Hands on the mainmast."

Fingers trembling with stupid, righteous fury, Jones removed his shirt and dropped it on the deck at his feet. Despite the numerous eyes on them both, he couldn't resist stealing one last glance at Nadia, white-faced and desperate and just out of reach. *I'm sorry*, he thought as he braced his hands against the wood. *I failed us both, not you.*

The lash whistled behind him, and Jones choked on his next breath as fire burned across his skin, a bright, searing pain that buried everything except the low, helpless sound of Nadia sobbing. He had no voice to comfort her and no strength to go to her—no strength for anything except breathing and trying to stay upright and trying not to howl like a wounded dog. Once the whip-crack of the last blow had faded, Jones slumped to his knees on the deck, fingers filling with splinters as he gripped the rough wood in an effort to stay conscious. The sound of Nadia's voice screaming his name rose in his ears.

"Harlan! Harlan!"

Dizzily, Jones looked up just in time to see them drag her below. He staggered to his feet, needing to get to her, to keep her safe. But the world shifted sharply in his field of vision, deck and sky slanting as a blackness deeper and wider than the ocean rose up to swallow him whole.

G. Z. Chapman

G. Z. Chapman spins fun fiction drawing from his life in mechanics, agriculture, restaurant & bar, programming, plumbing, business, consulting, writing, and devouring fiction, comics, and wikipedia. He once drove under a blinding UFO but it was probably ice zapping off high power lines.

BY SURF AND STONE
G. Z. Chapman

They glow in darkness
  Moon shines through them.
Dressed long ago
  Their clothes unchanged.
They wear their seaweed
  Like haute couture.
Walk across the ocean
  On roads not there.
From under stone
  He rises most tall
Evil grin claws
  They dance to his call.
Whirling and spinning,
  The winds start to howl.
Wrong path taken
  They cannot now depart.
Dawn approaches and
  They drown again
Their cold beds bind them
  In the depths chain them.
Each night they find shore
  Make port their bones cannot
Until world's breaking
  They cannot depart.

R.C. Davis

R.C. Davis is a writer of fiction and poetry, living in Iowa City, Iowa. While he grew up in the rolling hills that form the western banks of the Mississippi River, his interests in people, places, and genres are cosmopolitan in scope. With nine published works, find R.C. at www.rcdavis-tellinstories.com

Deepwater Metamorphosis
R.C. Davis

Harry and Debbie agreed to leave New Hampshire to return the thirty something miles down the Massachusetts coast to Winnie's place. Their friend and fellow monster slayer would be happy to see them again, but the joy wouldn't last. She would inquire about the absence of his father, and the jubilant reunion would dissolve into sorrow. Harry would try to explain how his father had stood his ground at Billy B's cottage, fighting the monsters to the very end. That would bring the tears, and possibly—the rage that Harry so wished to unleash on those cold-blooded fiends.

Debbie insisted on using Billy B's boat to cross Little Harbor. Someone had stripped the red gillnetter of its net drum and other fishing apparatus. Harry assumed Billy B. had used the old sternpicker for leisure at a time before the monsters appeared.

Crossing the harbor by boat would take a few extra miles off their trek, but at great risk. Debbie insisted it was safe enough, reminding him that the Thulu only hunted after dark and limited their daytime activity to the ocean; not inlets or bays. If Harry were to keep the boat at full throttle all the way across, they should be able to get to the other side before the pea-brains even knew the two of them were out there. He protested but gave in when she put on her pouty face. He could never tell her no, and she knew it.

Halfway across, the gillnetter ran out of

fuel. The gauge read half full, but when he tapped it with a finger, the red needle plummeted to 'E'. Finding a full can of gas stashed under a makeshift bench at the transom, he twisted off the cap to the boat's fuel tank and poured in the entire can.

Moving from the wheelhouse, Debbie sat on the gunwale where it met the transom. She chatted about all the things she would do when they got back to Winnie's. Harry, so preoccupied with his task and the irritation accompanying the circumstances, didn't think to remind Debbie that her choice of seats was a bad idea.

He hadn't even gotten the gas cap back on when the Thulu came straight up out of the water. At the apex of its skyward lunge, its dragon like wings opened and flapped, pummeling the two monster slayers with turbulent gusts of air. Torrents of water ran off its gleaming olive skin and the short tentacles at its mouth writhed as if in competition with each other.

Debbie cried, "Oh crap," and stood to run as the beast lowered its clawed feet down to the gunwale where she had been sitting. Its weight rocked the boat, causing Harry to fall, and Debbie to tumble backwards into the beast's outstretched arms.

Harry stared in shock and disbelief as the Thulu wrapped Debbie in a bear hug, pinning her arms to her sides. Her right hand still scrabbled to find the hilt of her sword, but the beast only squeezed her tighter to its simian-like body. Its whip of a tail jerked and snapped as the beast sent a loud hiss in Harry's direction, its large black eyes unblinking. The expression on Debbie's face was one of pure terror. A look he had never seen there before, but knew he would never forget.

His anger surged in, forcing out the fear. He tried to gain his feet, but the Thulu pushed off with such force that the gillnetter rocked low enough to take on water. The beast rose to hover, a hissing shriek filling the air. In its crushing grip, Debbie could only expel, "Harry," in a plaintive croak before the beast inverted and dove head first into the harbor.

The splash soaked him from head to foot and he took it as a contemptuous gesture. Finding his feet, he lowered his center of gravity and drew his butterfly swords. His first impulse was to dive in after them. When he realized that wouldn't help, he bellowed his hatred in the direction the sea monster had gone. A sense of helplessness was eking in, but he fought to keep it at bay. Wavering wasn't an option; he had to do something—anything.

He still stood dumbstruck, watching the ocean, his thoughts in turmoil as his brain sought a solution. Then the water boiled at the opening in the seawall. From the bubbling foam, something broke the surface—a human arm with flashing sword in hand.

Debbie's free and she's fighting!

The feeling of impotence that had enveloped him, dissolved away. He knew what he needed to do. Sheathing his blades, he returned to the wheelhouse. At the second press of the starter button, the engine came alive. Pushing the throttle forward to the 'Full' mark, he whipped the boat around and roared away to where Debbie's sword had broken the surface.

Slowing the boat to a crawl, he scanned the water, his eyes frantically searching, as he muttered, "Where are you, Debbie? Dammit! Where are you?"

Catching movement out of the corner of his eye, he brought his face around to see the water roil again farther out in the ocean. There flashed a hint of Debbie's blue and white plaid shirt and he sped the boat in that direction.

The sun glinting off the rippling surface made it difficult to determine where it had been. He brought the engine back to an idle and stepped to the window on the right side of the wheelhouse, shielding his eyes with a hand against the glare. Not finding anything starboard, he moved portside. A numbing shock ran up from his feet to the top of his head and his hair stood on end as bile rose in his throat. Pieces of Debbie's shirt swirled past in thinning clouds of crimson, agitated by the wake of the boat.

Harry lost his mind.

A deep chill enveloped his body and he shuddered as threats against every sea monster in existence resonated within that cabin. When the Thulu showed itself about a hundred yards off the bow, Harry slammed the throttle lever forward with such force, it bent, cracking the plastic housing around its base. Hopping anxiously from one foot to the other, he kept a white knuckled grip on the wheel. Curses, more typical of a longshoreman than a well-brought-up nineteen-year-old, poured from his mouth.

He glowered at the creature as it swam ahead, sometimes just a 'V' cutting through the waves, at other times, its folded wings and tail breaking just above them. The gillnetter was moving as fast it could, and it seemed to be closing the gap. But that wasn't fast enough for Harry.

Stepping back from the wheel, he bent forward at the waist and clenching his fists, he cut loose with a growling scream at the windshield. When he had spent his breath, he drew another, and raising his face and fists to the ceiling, he bellowed his rage.

Taking the wheel again, he steered after the Thulu who had changed its route to a more northerly direction. He went to stomping his right foot hard against the floor as if it would speed the process. Minutes passed, and his mumbled threats became punctuated with snarls of exasperation. The distance between him and the monster soon closed to about 100 yards, and within his madness, there came a transient rationality.

After tying the wheel in place with a short length of cord, he moved out onto the platform deck that ran from the door back to the stern. Yanking one of Billy B's homemade harpoons from its clamp, he scrambled around the outside of the wheelhouse to crouch on the prow deck. Finding the mooring line that snaked back from a cleat at the forward most point, Harry rose to his feet and pulled it taut with his left hand while holding the harpoon high at the ready with his right.

His russet hair whipped around his head and the spray doused him as he cried into the wind, "Come back here, you bastard! Come take me! I'm right here, you… you son of a…" His voice cracked as he struggled to see through wind and tear-filled eyes. He offered himself to the Thulu again and again, hoping it would turn back. But the tireless creature swam on, and Harry followed it far out into the Atlantic.

After a while he lost track of the Thulu and found he was only chasing waves. His head swiveled crazily from left to right and back again as his eyes scanned for anything that might be a sign of the creature. He jabbed at the air and continued with his threats, each one slightly different and louder than the last. Soon, like his mind, Harry lost his voice.

The engine began to smoke long before that point. At first, little wisps came filtering out of the compartment's cover. They soon evolved into a heavy, black cloud that rose skyward to trail out far behind the boat. Harry failed to notice as he stomped back and forth across the prow deck, twice nearly tumbling over the edge.

Ten minutes passed, fifteen, and then twenty, the lighthouse becoming just a mere speck in the distance. But time no longer mattered to Harry. The mind he lost—the one that he possessed back in hometown Massachusetts—had actually been stolen. The theft had been a gradual process, starting with the loss of his mother, followed by his father, and now, Debbie. The mutated H1N1 pandemic of 2032, climate change, and the monsters, were all culprits in the thievery.

He would not forget the overwhelming despair as he watched the 'Bug' claim friends and family while decimating over two thirds of the world's population. Then there was the cataclysmic weather which brought such a sense of powerlessness that he supposed only a child caught up in war could fear worse.

However, he was quite capable of driving a sword or spear into the guts of some abhorrent sea monster. That's where he dominated. It appealed to something deep down inside him—a primal thing.

It was a caveman that rode that boat like a mad surfer.

When the engine seized, and the boat became enslaved by the waves, Harry fell to his knees, sobs racking his body. Clinging to the harpoon, he tilted his head back and wailed up into the azure void. His nose flowed freely, and saliva ran from the corners of his mouth as he rocked back and forth rasping out, "Come take me… please… come take me."

The monster never came back. Nor did any other respond to Harry's invitation. So, moving to sit cross-legged, he cradled the shaft of the long, barbed weapon in his arms and bobbed along with the boat, weeping. The breeze cooled him in his wet clothes as he struggled to push the picture of Debbie's fear-filled face out of his head. But it kept coming back. The look of terror in her eyes said, "Only you can save me now," and he had failed her.

It was hard to take. He just wanted to stop caring, to be devoid of emotion. He wanted to sleep a long, dreamless slumber from which there would be no awakening.

Laying down, he pulled the harpoon close to his side and pushed his feet back toward the windscreen. Closing his eyes, he mumbled to himself, incoherent babbling perpetuated by the images cycling through his head.

Winnie's face soon appeared, bringing a halt to the endless reel of memories. From her lips came the words spoken at their parting, *"Take care of them, Harry."* He promised he would, and he had botched it. Muttering a mournful, "I'm sorry," he drifted off into a fitful sleep.

***

It was dark when he woke himself shouting, "Debbie, look out!" With a fire in his throat, he looked around in confusion. His sorrow and regret stampeded in like a herd of wild buffalo. He remembered where he was, and regrettably, that he was still alive.

There was a terrible pain in his gut and his chest felt heavy with heartache. The harpoon was gone. Searching the deck, he failed to find it and figured it had found its way to the ocean floor. So, he sat, scanning the sky, listening to the ocean's night voice. The moon was up and reflecting off the surface like a silvery finger pointing at him—the guilty party.

He rocked with the waves, wondering what he should do next. It occurred to him to lash the anchor to his body and jump overboard. But that's not how he wanted to go. It had to be in battle—nothing else.

Debbie kept tiptoeing into his head like a specter from the shadows. But Harry was all cried out. So, the images and the words she left behind whirled like a dust devil inside his skull. He still could not fathom that, one minute they were just talking, and the next— she was gone.

Debbie's gone.

With a stuttering sigh, he moved back to the main deck. He needed water, and his head was splitting as if someone had cleaved it with one of his swords. Sitting down on the bench outside the wheelhouse door, he dragged Debbie's backpack to him and opened the flap. Pulling out a plastic water bottle, he uncapped it and drank. Then setting it aside, he found the little flashlight he had given her, and turning it on, he held it in his lips while removing other items from the bag. There were cans of food, more bottles of water, clothing, little personal things, a sharpening stone, a Swiss Army knife, and—her wallet. He wanted to look inside, but…

Should I wait? No—better to get it over with.

Flipping it open, a photo fell out. Picking it up, he saw it was a picture of him and her together after a tournament win at the 2029 Boston Marital Arts Expo.

He was standing with Debbie seated on his outstretched arm, her feet dangling. She had one arm around his neck and in her other hand, a trophy held high in the air, her head thrown back in glee. Strands of auburn hair covered her face disclosing only part of her toothy smile. He remembered spinning her around afterwards, and losing his balance, they tumbled to the mat in laughter.

In the background, he could see Master Bik shaking hands with his mother and father. They had all been there on that joy-filled day, and now—they were all gone. He was alone, and that was something he had rarely ever been.

He found he still had one teardrop left as it fell onto the photo. Wiping it away, he pushed the picture under his leg to keep the breeze from stealing his treasure. Inspecting the rest of the wallet's contents and finding nothing but a bunch of defunct plastic cards, he stuffed it and the other things he couldn't use, back inside the pack. Flinging it aft, he watched it fall onto a coil of rope and bump the empty gas can to send it spinning away into a corner.

The flashlight soon offered nothing but a meager glow. He rapped it on the wall behind him and when the beam did not return to full strength, he grew annoyed. Flinging it high into the air, he smirked when he heard it splash. Then in frustration, he stood and stomped across the deck to Debbie's bag and flung it in as well. It twirled away with somewhat of a whistling noise, making an odd *smack!* when it hit the water.

He stood gazing in the direction that it had gone, smelling the ocean's salty breath, and listening to the waves lap the hull.

Maybe that was a bad idea?

He felt screwed, regardless. Yet, he needed to holdout until a monster showed up to grant him his final showdown. He figured he could make his drinking water last a couple weeks, thanks to Debbie's stubbornness. She'd packed more bottles than he thought they needed. He had given her crap for it, but she persevered. Now, he was glad for her foresight and he so wished he could tell her.

He was also the unhappy recipient of her share of the food. If he was prudent, he might make it last as long as the water supply. Fishing could offer another source of food, but he didn't like fish. However, he could change his mind if it became necessary. Time would be the deciding factor.

The thought of it being more acceptable for a sea creature to eat him than for him to eat a sea creature, brought a crazy little laugh to his lips, and shaking his head, he moved back toward the wheelhouse. He spied the photo he'd left behind and there came a hint of panic at realizing he could have easily lost it to the ocean. Snatching it up, he stuffed it in his back pocket and went inside the wheelhouse.

Moonlight gleamed off the large red 'STARTER' button and he gave it a quick push just to be sure. The relay sent out a staccato of clicks, but nothing turned. Running full tilt for that great of a distance, the engine had succumbed to his abuse. There was no way to row or pole the boat. A sail could be rigged, but he had no idea how to work such a thing. He would remain adrift on the Atlantic until the sea monsters came, he died from exposure—or found land.

The chance that someone may just show up was a reoccurring thought, but a stupid one at that. There would be no one searching for him. He was on his own. It made him think about those old movies he watched as a kid where sailors had gotten lost at sea, floating for months on a little rubber dinghy. He remembered the trepidation he felt for those fictitious characters. Yet, always at the back of his mind, he knew he was safe sitting there in his living room. What someone acted out on the silver screen was hardly real life. He could only assume what would come in the days ahead.

He thought again about drowning himself, but with even greater revulsion than the first time. The cowardice of it took him back to an episode in the third grade at Kilbury elementary. Jimmy Jamison threatened to beat the crap out of him and it sent him fleeing to hide in the janitor's closet. The event had been the motivation behind joining Master Bik's Kung Fu academy. He vowed to himself that he would never run again.

"Better to go down fighting," he mumbled to himself as he stood leaning with both hands flat on the control panel. The loneliness was already creeping in and he sensed his isolation. The only thing he could compare it to was being stuck in the house on a rainy day with no one else home and nothing to do.

What are you going to do with yourself until the monsters come?

In a burst of anger, he pounded on the panel with a fist, yelling, "Dammit! Dammit! Dammit!" Then stepping over to the searchlight, he switched it on and shined it around on the water, shouting as loud as he could, "Here I am you bastards, time for supper!"

A burning sensation filled his throat as his words dwindled to a gruff whisper. The searchlight used the last of the battery's energy and its stream of light dissolved away into nothing. Stomping out, he pulled the second harpoon from its stays and moved to the starboard side. Listlessly splashing the barbed tip in the water, he watched the lightning play among the thunderheads of a storm well far to the south.

The monsters aren't coming you idiot! Why can't you get it through your thick head?

A strange kind of lethargy overtook him. Putting the harpoon back in its clamps, he grabbed his bottle of water and sat down on the deck. After a long drink, he took off his sword rig and lay back. Pillowing his head on his arms, he gazed up into the celestial sphere. He thought maybe to eat something, but soon awoke to the dawn—and whatever had bumped against the bottom of the boat.

"What the…" he said with gravel in his voice.

Jumping to his feet, he strapped on his swords. Within seconds, the harpoon was back in his hands and at the ready. It was time to meet his death, and the adrenalin flowed in as he stood patient, waiting for the beast to show itself. He felt strangely lucid. His mind was back—but it wasn't his old one. This was his new mind, and it was clear, focused, and ready to go.

Time to face eternity.

He wished for the monster to have a clear view of him. So, he took up a position at the center of the deck, standing tall at arms, prepared for battle.

The sun soon peeked over the ocean's surface, but only for a few seconds before a narrow band of clouds hid it from view, casting Harry's world back into shadow. Remembering his own flashlight, he pulled it from his pocket. Sticking it in his mouth, he sent a beam of light in every direction he peered. He became a walking lighthouse, making damn sure the monster knew just where to find him.

The tiny stream of light played over the surface and he watched as a huge, dark shape passed underneath, rocking the boat. Harry waited for it to return, and when it did, its back split the surface. A dark hump, speckled with large whitish spots now cut through the water as it cruised toward him. His brain went into overdrive as he tried to figure out what type of creature had arrived to help end his pain.

He couldn't recall anything with white spots like that. But there were new monsters showing up almost daily, beasts that had not made it into the Government's, 'Extrinsic Biological Aberrations-Identification Manual'. His father had stolen a copy from an Army transport and Harry had studied it with diligence every night after.

When the spotted hump was about ten feet from the boat, his instincts told him to throw the harpoon—but he hesitated. He wanted the satisfaction of having his hands on the shaft as he drove it home. Moving to the portside, he waited to jump on the beast when it appeared. He would use all his weight to push the barbed lance clear up to the wooden haft. Then he would take out his swords and go to work on whatever it was; least until it killed him, or he drowned. But the creature dove deeper just before reaching the gillnetter, and he could no longer see it.

It'll come back. No way the bastard's going to let me escape.

Harry braced himself for the jump, holding the harpoon high above his head with both hands, the tip angled down toward the water.

This is it! The moment I become history!

He was afraid, but also—excited. That was good. It was just what he wanted.

The sensation was much different from what he had experienced when confronting other monsters. Those times when his father was looking on, Debbie standing by, ready to jump in. He wanted to impress them. Make them see he was good at this. He hadn't truly felt the finality of what his actions could bring. He never thought he might die, and now, he was so willing to make sure he didn't survive.

"Come back here, you son of a bitch. You're making me wait."

The creature breached the surface a short way out from the boat, its full length breaking free of the water. Confusion rolled in and Harry relaxed his grip on the harpoon.

A freaking whale!

The young Humpback splashed down and turned toward him, gliding just inches below the surface. He had seen a live whale only once. It had been on a visit to the beach as a little boy. Everyone around him had grown excited as they watched through binoculars. He remembered his father supporting their pair, so Harry could get a glimpse. The common belief was that all whales had gone extinct, killed by human beings, or sea monsters. But this one had obviously beaten the odds.

When it arrived at the gillnetter, it floated to a stop and turned parallel, rolling over onto its side. The beam of the flashlight rested on one large eye as it checked him out. He dropped the harpoon and stared back, wondering what was going on inside the

Humpback's head. He suspected it was just as amazed as he was. A mammal meeting another in a world of amphibious mutants.

It seemed something passed between them. A mammalian kind of telepathy. "Happy to see you've made it this far!" formed in large, white letters running panoramic across his mind's eye. Harry scowled in disbelief. But his skepticism didn't last because he so wanted to believe he had made a connection. Taking the flashlight from his mouth, he dropped to his knees. Pressing his chest against the gunwale, he stretched out a hand and placed his palm flat against the strange, wet roughness of the whale's skin.

They remained that way for all of ten seconds. Then the whale fell away into the depths and Harry thought it gone. "Good luck, you're going to need it," he monotoned, the hoarseness of his voice sounding strange in the breezy, morning air.

As Harry turned away, the whale breached the ocean's surface a few hundred yards out. He turned to see it spiral toward the sky as if in a leap of joy at simply being alive. The sun broke through the clouds and the great creature glimmered in its light. A warm sensation blossomed within him, and surprisingly—it felt a lot like hope.

Laurie Penland

With 30 years as a professional photographer and Scuba Diver, Laurie Penland's love for the underwater realm is realized in her current position as a Smithsonian Diving Officer. Penland is writing a cli-fi novel, a culmination of her personal journey through life and her concerns for the future of this planet.

The Reclamation
Laurie M. Penland

A deep red sunrise turned the ocean into a sea of blood as the engines spewed out a boiling froth from under the stern. Fuel mixed noxiously with the stench of decay. Two deckhands admired the morning's first haul. On the catch table, an occasional fish flopped--gasping for life--among the by-catch of trash. Most of the other fish on the table were mercifully dead. Their blood-filled eyes bulged and their stomachs--inside-out like plastic bags--protruded from their mouths, a result of the decompression from being dragged up from the depths of the ocean.

"You see that?" Bob asked. The raspy twang in his voice betrayed harsh days from a southern past. His bulging eyes were reminiscent of the dead fish on the table and equally reddened, but from the weed he was smoking. He leaned over the gunnel and looked toward the bow.

"Nope." With a long inhale, José took a hit off the joint, held it in, then passed the joint back to Bob. José exhaled as he ran a filthy hand through his thick black hair. He picked up a dead fish off the floor, threw it overboard, and watched it disappear. With surprising stability José walked across the rolling deck to examine the catch table. He picked up an old shoe and threw it overboard, then prodded at a fish, trying to shove its stomach back where it belonged.

"What'd you do that for?" Bob asked, and then inhaled.

"Que?"

Bob's eyes bulged even more as he held it in.

"Trashed the water?" he said as he exhaled a lungful of smoke.

"Mucho basura," José said. "Old shoe no es importa."

José returned to poking the fish. Bob watched the shoe drift off, then disappear in a swarm of bubbles.

Then they disappeared.

The Government wasn't alarmed. Ships "disappear these days" for a multitude of reasons, debris entanglement, rogue waves from distant storms. A sinking ship was no longer an oddity. But when they found this one at the bottom of the channel, it was completely absent of the crew.

"ENTIRE SHIP CREW SWALLOWED ALIVE BY SEA MONSTER!" the fake news said. People panicked.

The White House tweeted: "We are unaware of any man-eating Sea Monsters. In fact, what is The President having for dinner tonight? Seafood."

***

Tony made this trip once a week. It was his favorite route. Something about being by the shore lifted his spirit—made him feel free—compared to the confines of the city. At times the morning sun blinded his view as he headed east, but he knew the way. The first stop was a town called Bethany. He loved the name and dreamed of retiring in this tiny town on the coast.

Tony's fantasies included someone

delivering him packages to his house on the beach. Maybe not directly on the beach. Hurricanes and sea level rise had moved houses inland once already. Maybe he would live near the coast and make this drive every day, just for fun.

Maybe he had taken a wrong turn.

Nothing looked familiar. He should have been there by now. The town should have been right in front of him. Maybe it was—just under the debris which now blocked his way. He thought could see pieces of the boardwalk sticking out like broken ribs.

Tony climbed out of his delivery truck.

The air was silent. Nothing moved.

He decided to walk into town to find some help. He still had packages to deliver and couldn't carry them by himself. Whatever happened, it wasn't his fault, and he needed to keep his job if he was ever going to retire.

The only possible path was on the beach, so that was where he headed. Strange marks in the sand worked their way from the rubble into the water. Tony used to drive a tractor-trailer in his early days. He was more important then, delivering large shipments across the country. Entire stores depended on him. These tracks reminded Tony of his truck. He missed those days.

Following the tracks toward the ocean, Tony realized that something was missing. Amplified by the silence, waves thundered onto the beach. He reached the waterline and watched miscellaneous debris roll back and forth. An occasional curiosity--a hairbrush, a toy boat--was left behind with the receding tide.

"Where are the people?" he said out loud. Then he too disappeared.

"ENTIRE VILLAGE SWALLOWED ALIVE BY A SEA MONSTER!" the fake news cried.

The White House tweeted: "a super-tide overwhelmed the village and pulled it into the sea, then returned the village in ruins. Sad!" There was no explanation for why the people didn't return.

Nearby coastal towns scratched their heads. They hadn't experienced anything like a super-tide. And the moon was just after its quarter-when they have neap tides—so the water level changes were minimal. And those tractor marks along the beach? The locals knew water didn't rise that high and if it did, the waves would have washed the tracks away.

"SEA MONSTER TRACKS FOUND ON BEACH AFTER SWALLOWING ENTIRE VILLAGE!" the fake news screamed.

The White House smiled and issued another tweet: "Sea monsters don't leave tracks, they swim!"

***

His tiny feet carried him ahead of his mom, smacking with satisfaction in the wet sand.

"Stay away from the water, Elijah!" his mom yelled. He stopped to looked around. The breeze on his face made him giggle. Waves were crashing far away and his mom was still in sight, so he ran on.

Elijah dodged the plastic debris as it washed ashore. It became a game, running, splashing, and dodging debris when the water rushed beneath him. The footprints he left behind washed away with every receding wave.

Something shiny washed up. It started to bounce along in front of him so he had to chase it. It stopped bouncing so he could get close, then took off again. Elijah squealed with delight.

"What is it, Elijah?"

He was too far from her. She started to run.

This time when it stopped, he caught up to it. The shiny green orb reflected his face and distorted it in silly ways. He burst out laughing, reached down, and picked it up.

All of his footprints disappeared.

"SMALL CHILD LURED INTO THE SEA AND SWALLOWED ALIVE BY THE SEA MONSTER!" the fake news shouted.

The government searched the shoreline with unmanned drones and found nothing. The White House frowned and issued another tweet: "We are not responsible for silly unwatched free-range kids who run into the ocean."

***

At a lab in Delaware, a grad student watched in horror as her beloved cetaceans were vilified by the terrified public. She had diligently studied cetacean mortality rates in relation to shipping routes for years and knew that whales, not humans, were the true victims.

There will be whaling ships with harpoons again if this keeps up, she thought.

The student followed a hunch and reversed the data. She ran computer models on ship mortality rates in relation to cetacean migration patterns and began to notice something interesting. Along the migration and shipping routes, cetacean mortality rates were inversely proportional to ship mortality rates.

In other words, there was a decrease in whale deaths (and an overall increase in marine life) when and where there was an increase in sinking ships.

That's correlation, not causation.

***

The coastal cities, towns, and villages were now completely abandoned; they looked like a wasteland of garbage dumps. Politicians across the world blamed their enemies. Their enemies, in return, blamed them. This was happening to everyone, everywhere. The only countries not directly hit were countries with no coastal borders. The people knew it was not political.

But to politicians, everything was political.

Eventually ships were disappearing at such an alarming rate that insurance companies filed for bankruptcy. All ocean shipping stopped. Open-water recreational activities ceased, bringing the tourist industry to a complete halt. No one would go near the ocean.

***

The Reclamation

The ensuing absence of ocean activity left only the enduring voices of academics and grad students. Once they began to compare data, a picture emerged. Something in the ocean had definitely changed.

Ship mayday recordings, cetacean hydrophone recordings, all underwater recordings, were re-evaluated. The Channel 16 VHF mayday calls were short and similar. "Mayday Mayday! We are sinking, we are--"

Whatever was happening was happening fast.

One student noticed a distinct change in the auditory rhythm arrays. With the absence of human noises, new patterns emerged. Marine mammals seemed to be interacting with other marine life. The students all agreed that the conclusion was anthropomorphic, but it seemed to them as if the shrimp were clapping at the end of an unusually long dolphin "lecture". To their fascination, it sounded like interspecies communication.

***

Mountains of plastic debris began to appear along the coast. Satellite images showed a wall forming. The government bulldozed it all right back into the sea, only to have it re-emerge the next morning. Then one by one, sunken ships began to appear on the beaches. No one knew how. It was as if someone was cleaning up the ocean and dumping everything onto the land.

***

The professor climbed over the sea of debris that used to be her oceanfront home in Cape May, Delaware.

They're weaving algae into nets now, very impressive.

A bedraggled mat of soggy orange fuzz--once a beautiful cat called Tabitha--was ensnared in a strangely structured mass of algae. Tabitha was bycatch.

It was her grad students who were pouring over data from the subsea near-shore cameras. Visibility was so bad that no one looked at visual data anymore. But the audio wasn't convincing enough. They *needed* a visual.

When a grad student first saw it, his stomach lurched and his heart broke. Even through the low visibility, it was perfectly clear; once they knew what to look for, it was easy to find.

Crabs hanging out on pilings weren't eating their usual diet. Instead, they picked at human remains. Sharks, rays, large fish--all the top predators--were fighting over human bodies. A dolphin, caught on camera, was dragging the arm of a human in its teeth and laughing. The students piled around to watch the footage, over and over again.

"Heck, if I was them I'd be doing it too," one student said.

The professor's lab released a statement: AVAILABLE DATA ASSOCIATED WITH DISAPPEARING HUMANS IN COASTAL REGIONS (DHCR) SUGGESTS THAT DHCR IS A RESULT OF TARGETED HUMAN CONSUMPTION BY MARINE LIFE.

"SEA MONSTER SCARE IS A GOVERNMENT PLOT TO TAKE OVER THE ENTIRE COAST. STAND YOUR GROUND." the fake news shouted.

The White House issued a new tweet: "Sea Monsters are as difficult to prove as they are to disprove..."

***

Somewhere deep beneath the waves, in the safe, clean, and peaceful ocean, a giant pacific octopus rolled a human skull onto the pile of bones just outside her lair. Sitting at the entrance, she looked out at the small village of fellow cephalopods in her underwater world, and smiled.

J. E. Brooke

J. E. Brooke is a public health anthropologist by day, fantasy writer by night. When she isn't writing stories and novels about mermaids and dragons, she can be found knitting or cross stitching, cooking delicious food, or lost in the pages of a good book. She lives in Iowa City.

Silver and Syrup

J. E. Brooke

Arui watched the passage of foot traffic in and out of the city from the top of the shallow hill, over the tops of hundreds and hundreds of faded scrap-cloth tents pitched on the dry scrub. Alabaster nobles dressed in splendid light summer tunics of silk and linen showed their citizens' sigils to the grim-looking watchmen and were allowed to pass with a polite bow of respect. There was a small crowd of Alabasters already, eager to gawk at the passing Strangers while pointedly ignoring the children who approached them asking for food or coins, or to proselytize and give alms the beach-dwellers to please the Juranian god. Brick-caste merchants passed through the gate, too; not so finely dressed as their Alabaster superiors, but lugging carts and sacks laden with goods to sell at the Invisible Market just to the west of the gate. The watchmen took no notice of the illegal sale and barter of city goods at exorbitant prices to Strangers. For the right price, of course.

The Strangers passing by were careful to keep their distance of the gate and its keepers, who would brandish their meticulously sharpened and polished swords and spears menacingly if they perceived a Stranger stepped too close. The sight of the watchmen and their weapons sent Arui's brain spinning without warning to the night before, hearing again the ragged breaths of her parents' newest patient as they washed her bruised and lacerated skin as gently as they could. But even gentleness couldn't prevent the screams of pain that followed. The noisy white crescents of gulls and turns arced overhead, breaking the hold of the memory. Arui blinked rapidly, and remembered where she was.

The narrow span of the world between sea and stone walls was silent for the moment. That would change shortly, when the scores of Stranger families living on the beach outside the grey stone walls of Jurinar broke down their homes to wash them clean in the salty seawater. Wash day was as close to a holiday as the Feast of Death and the Day of the Pale Lord that had been foisted upon them by the Alabaster nobles. Though the communal washing wasn't a holy day, it frequently had the air of a carnival, neighbors working and laughing side by side in shin-deep brackish tidal inlets just to the west of the Invisible Market as their children splashed and shrieked happily through the waves.

Arui, though, at eleven years of age had no time for such babyish pursuits today, although it would help keep anyone who could stop her distracted from doing so. She kicked the heel of a bare foot into the sand, scattering the grains backward onto the scraggly grass, and then spotted Tominae running toward her from among the rows of patchwork tents. Arui thrust her right arm as high as it would go and waved it determinedly so her friend would find her, raising herself up onto her toes for a little extra height. Tominae saw her and grinned, sprinting the remaining distance between them and kicking up sand in her hurry. "Hi Arui," the girl said laughingly.

Arui smirked a little. "You're late. I was going to come looking for you if you didn't get here soon. I thought you might still be sleeping."

"Jora woke up just as I was leaving and asked me for a sweet in exchange for not telling our parents I was sneaking out. It's embarrassing, being ransomed by a seven-year-old. Little sisters are the worst. You're so lucky you're an only child, Rui."

"That I know of," Arui replied as they slipped out of the tent encampment toward the far end of the beach. The high outermost wall of the city loomed above them, rising to meet the slopes of the hills of Jurinar that ended abruptly in staggering cliffs the color of spent charcoal. The doleful cries of the birds who nested there could just be heard above the roar of waves crashing into the base of the outcropping.

"Did Finia or Laken catch you out for trying to sneak away," Tominae asked, and Arui laughed.

"You know them, too preoccupied being healers to bother with me," she replied, trying to ignore the small heaviness in her gut even as she tried to joke it away. "They only notice that I'm missing if I don't turn up for a healing lesson, or to help them in the clinic when I'm supposed to."

"That sounds lonely," Tominae said softly.

"It isn't so bad," Arui said. Tominae had a younger sister and brother, and her parents were talented drift carvers who sculpted pieces out of flotsam to sell to Alabaster gawkers and trade with other Strangers from their home. Laken and Finia were only her foster parents, and while they cared for her in their own way, their healing work occupied them during the day and often well into the evening so she was often alone. For a moment, Arui envied her friend that she only had to imagine loneliness, and not live with it, but the jealousy quickly passed as her focus returned to their mission. "Besides, it's useful for what we're going to do today."

She gave a pointed look up to the gray escarpment looming above them, the peaks and spires of Jurinar's noble central city circle almost obscured by the sheer rock face. The grinding smash of waves hitting the base of the outcropping grew louder as they neared. Great whitecaps slammed themselves against it and broke, sending spray high into the air and raining down again to give the cliffs a grim shine. This part of the beach was usually unoccupied, but that didn't eliminate the possibility of a city watchman on a slow day taking a stroll in hopes of arresting a Stranger to fill his quota. Shouting over the sea could get them caught, so they switched to sign.

It looks calmer, Rui signaled to Tominae and pointed to a spot on the beach nearby where the water lapped quietly over the sand. The current would grow more hostile as they drew nearer to the rocks. *We should go in there.*

Are you sure about this, *Rui*, Tominae asked hesitantly. If no one else has found the cavern in all these years, what makes you think we're going to?

We're braver than the rest of them, Arui smirked, and approached the water. Tominae followed closely behind, and they waded into the cold sea up to their waists before plunging under the surface of the water.

Arui felt the skin on her neck part slowly as it sensed the salty water surrounding them.

Her cilia unfurled themselves from between the slits; short, iridescent blue fronds that turned pink as they absorbed oxygen from the water and carried it through the rest of her body. She opened her eyes and looked around, vision blurry at first but clearing rapidly as her clear secondary eyelids slid moved into place. Tominae was an arm's length away, eyes closed and smiling rapturously at the feeling of cold water moving over her fronds. Arui smiled and reached for her friend's hand. They had to start moving.

Ages ago, the Alabaster nobility of Jurinar built a shrine to their death god in the base of the escarpment, and filled it with surrendered treasures as offerings. The sea didn't drown the rocks then, but then over time the water rose and the temple was submerged. Alabasters had no talent for breathing water, and so their treasures were lost. Now and then, young Strangers would dare each other to find the lost temple and seize the riches that were said to be waiting there, but they were always stopped by their own fear, or a wizened elder who knew better, or in the worst cases a city watchman who caught wind of what they were discussing. For a Stranger, even talk was deadly when it dealt with crossing the Alabasters. Only in the sea, away from the walls and oppression of the city, could the Strangers find freedom, Arui was certain. Their talent had helped them survive their entrapment for centuries, ever since their initial banishment from the city, allowing them to fish and harvest enough to sustain themselves from the nearby seafloor. If only they could use it to escape for good.

No one quite knew how the Strangers came to have their particular talent. Some stories said they were being compensated by the gods for their harsh treatment by the people of Jurinar, demonized, denied citizenship, and forced to eke out an existence just beyond on the precarious boundary of scrub and beach between sea. Others told of a people of fishfolk who one day came ashore and intermarried with the land-living people they found there, only to be displaced by the Juranians. Her guardians dismissed both as fanciful thinking. "We've simply developed along the path the gods set for us long ago," her foster mother, Finia, replied once after Arui had asked. "Divine compensation and fish folk have nothing to do with it." Whatever the reason she had them, Arui was glad to have her fronds now. She was one of the strongest swimmers in the Stranger encampment, even among the adults. The gift of breathing water was unevenly given among her people, or else they would have all swam away by now. Some could do it for an hour or two, and others not at all, and every variation in between. Arui had yet to find her limit, so she tested it as often as she could. Tominae was an average swimmer, which for a Stranger was still superior to their city counterparts, and could only stay underwater for about an hour before she began to choke and gag and needed to surface again, but she could keep up, and Arui wanted her best friend at her side to share in this adventure.

The two girls swam out into the deep water and turned towards the submerged base of the escarpment. The sea floor below them was jagged with rocks and coral, teeming with small iridescent fish darting to find shelter among the innumerable cracks and crevices. Arui swam ahead, trusting that her friend would keep up. She closed her eyes again and relished the feel of water on her bare face and hands. Her fitted clothing only felt a little heavier for being soaked through and were still loose enough that she didn't feel restricted in her broad, smooth strokes through the water. She wanted to float here in the beautiful sea forever, far away it seemed from the land and its cities and Alabasters, watchmen and foster parents. Here away from all of that with Tominae…

Whose fronds would give out before long, an annoyingly practical voice that sounded a great deal like Finia's reminded her flatly from the back of her mind. Arui sighed a little and opened her eyes, accelerating her movements through the water. She casually turned around to sign to Tominae that they should hurry, because there was no guarantee that the temple cave would have any air for her when they found it. But the other girl wasn't behind her anymore, or within her field of vision at all. Trying not to panic, Arui scanned the water before her for any sign of her friend. Then, she looked down and felt horror bloom in her stomach at the sight of Tominae wrapped tightly in a long, undulating mauve tentacle. Her friend struggled to break free even as she was being pulled down into the coral bed by the terrible mighty appendage, beating and clawing and finally even biting down on the rubbery flesh. The tentacle didn't relinquish its hold, but started to reel from side to side as it slid down beneath the fissures in the coral and rock, coming dangerously close to striking Tominae with them. Trying to incapacitate its prey.

A gurgling cry tore from Arui's mouth as she hurled herself toward the creature, drawing the small sharp knife from its sheath tied to her ankle. She wrapped herself tightly around the tentacle just below where it held Tominae, and stabbed in viciously a dozen times before finally planting the blade deep and sawing back through the flesh until the great arm was in two pieces. There was a pained squeal from below the reef, followed by a tremor that shook the coral and stone as the creature fled in the opposite direction. The monstrous limb was still wrapped around Tominae as she fought to get loose, inky blue blood trailing into the water from the severed flesh. Arui swam frantically around her friend, gritting her teeth as she tried to think of a way to free the other girl.

Stabbing at the tentacle would risk hitting Tominae, reducing the knife to a deadly hindrance. Arui sheathed it and tried to pull the narrow end that had wrapped itself around her friend's neck, smothering her fronds. Tominae's movements grew slower, more languid as she suffocated. Arui pulled at the tentacle, digging her fingernails deep in the squelching flesh. More blue ink leaked out from the wounds she left into the water, but the appendage held fast, squeezing the life out of its prisoner. Desperately, she struck at the tentacle with her bare hands, punching as hard as she could through the drag of the sea. Nothing happened at first as her fists continued to hit, but then the constricting stopped and then, amazingly, reversed. The tentacle unwound slowly and dropped down to the coral below. Tominae fell slowly with it.

Arui grabbed her unconscious friend by the hand and lifted her back up into her arms, silently pleading with her to wake up as she swam with all her strength to reach the surface. A moment later they broke through, Tominae still insensible in her arms. "Tomi! Tominae, please wake up! I was so stupid to come out here, I'm so sorry." The girl shook her friend as she pleaded with her limp form. She didn't notice how they both drifted towards the sound of crashing waves, or how close the Jurinar escarpment was until they were almost before it. The roar of the water slamming into the rocks broke Arui out of her bargaining and she turned around to see the sheer rock face directly in front of them. The current was drawing them in. She struggled forward, trying to get away, but the force of the tide was too swift for Arui to fight while she carried her unconscious friend. They were both going to be broken against the stone precipice. Unable to think of another option, she pulled them both back under the water and swam down along the wall of rock, trying to find a way to escape the current that had ensnared them. Suddenly, the wall opened into a large cave. Without thinking of anything beyond helping her friend, Arui swam into a pitch-black tunnel leading upwards. Her eyes adjusted gradually to the murk around them. She swam as quickly as her tiring body would allow, taking care not to graze against the rock that surrounded them, harming Tominae further. Guilt and regret hammered in her head, throbbing with her pulse. This is my fault, my fault, my fault. I'm so sorry, don't die, don't die, don't die. Without warning, Arui's head broke through the water and into dank, humid air. She could see the faint outline of a ledge an arm's length to her right. Wearily, she hauled Tominae with her in the water, grabbed onto the wet, gritty stone, and held on.

A short eternity later, Tominae jerked lightly in Arui's arms and mumbled her name. Arui almost cried out, but managed to swallow the noise back down. Tominae grew more alert as the minutes passed, and before long she was able to hoist herself out of the water and onto the surrounding stone floor with Arui's help, coughing a little as her fronds closed on contact with the air. Then she collapsed and lay still. The other girl scrambled out and onto the ledge next to her friend, listening quietly. A moment later, Arui signed with relief. Tominae was still breathing.

"How do you feel," Arui asked.

"Sore," Tominae said hoarsely. "And tired."

"I'm sorry," Arui replied, blinking back tears. She was glad it was too dark for anyone to see her cry. "This was an awful idea."

"Told you so," Tominae said softly, and it took Arui a moment to realize that it was a joke. "Where are we now?"

"I'm not sure," Arui looked around, but it was too dark for even Stranger eyes to see more than a dim outline. "We got caught in a rip current after the monster let you go. I had to swim us into a cave before we got splattered against the rocks. I'm not sure where we came out." She stood, took a step away from her friend and accidentally stepped in a shallow pool in the rock. She pulled her foot back quickly in surprise, and gasped in amazement as the pool began to glow. She'd heard about pieces of light that scattered and moved in the sea before, of course. Some said they were tiny creatures that were too small to be seen, but she didn't expect to find them here, or that the light they cast would be so strong! The glow illuminated a good portion of the cave to the point where Arui could see that the space in which they stood was carved and decorated with elaborate motifs and that in places the stone had been hollowed out into deep shelves and filled with--

Treasure. The pale green light from the pool glinted off of heaping piles of gold, silver and jewels stuffed into the sacrificial shelves. Nameless gods, they had found the temple in spite of everything! "Tominae," Arui called excitedly. "Can you stand up?"

"I think so," her friend replied, and then groaned as Arui heard her move. She turned around, but Tominae was already walking slowly towards her, her soft brown eyes widening as she came to the pool of light and she saw what had been revealed in the glow.

"We did it?"

"We did!" Arui smiled and walked to the nearest of the alcoves, stepping in more puddles and churning up more of the green light to illuminate the cavern. Her smile faded as she came closer to the glittering heap. The metal was dull with time and some of the less resistant alloys had been eaten through with rust, but those damaged pieces were far outnumbered by pristine trophies for the Pale Lord, payment for a safe journey through death into the afterlife. But there was something wrong with the undamaged treasures. Arui picked one up, her frown deepening as she inspected it, and then she threw it harshly to the ground. She repeated the same series of actions with a second object, then a third, throwing them to the ground in increasing frustration.

"Arui, what is it? What's the matter," Tominae asked timidly as she shuffled closer.

Arui wheeled around, angry and almost in tears. "We're scuttled, that's what," she shouted. "Netted and drowned! These blighted things are all marked! They've all had the names of the families who gave them etched into them so that the Pale Lord can know who to give his favor to. They're worse than worthless, they're deadly!"

"Why?"

"If we took even one and tried to sell it, it would look like we'd stolen it from one of those stupid stuffy Alabasters and then they'd lock us away and kill us for sure. Rid themselves of a couple of little Stranger thieves. Drowned souls," she cursed. "These things don't even belong to anyone anymore! Think of what all of this could buy for the Strangers they've stranded on that beach! Food and clean water. Medicine. My mother and father can't even treat that poor girl who was beaten by the watchmen for stepping closer to the gate than they liked. When her parents brought her to us yesterday, I thought, 'She's Jora's age'. But even as good as Laken and Finia are with healing, they still can't do more for her than keep her wounds clean because they can't afford the medical supplies in the Market, and there's no one else who would sell to them! Those Alabasters deny us everything! I should have known they would find a way to punish us, even in death. They take so much, I just wanted to take something back for once." Arui dropped the silver chalice she'd been waving in her fury, sank to the ground, and rested her forehead on her knees as she wrapped her arms tightly around herself. Tominae silently walked over and crouched beside her, putting an arm around her back and squeezing gently.

"How could you know," Tominae whispered.

"I should have," Arui insisted. "I feel so stupid. This was my idea and it's failed, and I don't even know if we'll be able to get out of this cave again between the monster in the reef and the tide."

"We'll think of something," Tominae suggested meekly, although she sounded uncertain even as she said the words herself. "Or someone will notice we're missing and come looking for us. When the others realize we're not in camp, they'll search the coast and find the cave."

"For you, maybe. Laken and Finia won't notice that I'm gone until nightfall at least. If anyone comes looking, it'll be for you."

"Oh, Rui." Both girls sat in silence for a time, neither knew how long. Finally, Tominae stood shakily and extended a hand to Arui.

"Tomi?"

"If we're going to be stuck here, we should at least see if there's another way out. Are you going to help me walk? It's your fault I got hurt after all." Tominae smiled a little.

"And I thought coming up with terrible ideas was my job," Arui retorted, but took her friend's hand and smiled too as she stood. Tominae leaned on her for support, her left arm curling down over Arui's left shoulder. Slowly, with one girl supporting the other, they followed the long narrow chamber back, with only the eerie glow of the green waterlight to guide their way. They passed dozens more stone alcoves, all stuffed full of monogramed treasures. Arui's heart sank with each glimpse of another horde, until Tominae gasped.

"What? Are you hurt?"

"Rui, look!" With her free hand, Tominae pointed to a dimly lit corner. They had reached the back of the temple cavern, a smooth wall of stone--interrupted only by a fissure that looked like it might just be large enough for them to pass through. Arui thought that she saw a faint glow of white light, but didn't trust her eyes.

"Do you think it's a way out?" she asked.

"It's not like things could get," Tominae started to say, but Arui interrupted.

"I'm going to stop you right there," she said seriously. "I think I know how that sentence was going to end, and I don't want us jinxed on top of everything else."

Tominae replied, "Very well, but I do think we should try it."

"Are you sure you're up for it," Arui asked. "You're not hurt?"

"Nothing serious that I can feel yet," Tominae answered. She took a step toward the narrow aperture and winced. "Although I think I might already have some bruises from that creature."

"You should let me go first," Arui suggested. "That way I'll be the one in trouble if anything goes wrong in there." She walked towards her friend and stubbed her foot against a small hard lump on the ground. Arui's quick yelp echoed through the green-dark. It hadn't hurt exactly, but she was more surprised by the object's collision with her foot than anything. She bent down and picked up a small round pouch. The bag was leather, and yet amazingly preserved for having spent the last few centuries in a humid cave. She loosened the drawstring and smiled at the gold, silver, and copper pips she found inside. Nuggets of such raw precious metal were invaluable to a Stranger. Jurinar officially had a currency imposed by the Alabaster elites. However, like most other things of value it was forbidden to Strangers, and outside the city walls and even in the lower quarters the small nuggets could be traded for goods without jeopardizing the buyer by alerting the city watchmen. The other treasures here might be useless to her, but at least Arui would not leave empty handed after putting so much at risk.

Grinning, she showed Tominae, who broke into a wide grin as well. Arui pulled the drawstring shut on the bag and tied it to her belt, rebalanced herself, and slid into the fissure. The passage was wide enough for a child to pass through, but only just, and it was full of jagged edges of rock that caught and scraped, and sudden turns that narrowed ominously so that she almost had to slide sideways with her belly pressed against the stone wall. But it was also growing lighter with each step forward, and in another few moments she emerged in blinding white light, surrounded by warmth as her feet sank a little into soft, hot sand. She huffed a short laugh in relief. She was out!

Arui looked around as her eyes adjusted to the light. The tunnel had led her out to where the escarpment on the beach met with the highest part of the Jurinar wall. The aperture was visible to passersby, but narrow fissure was likely small enough that it didn't seem to be a potential liability to the rare watchman posted on this patrol. After all, the Alabaster ring of the city was high above, well protected and out of reach. The beach was deserted except for herself, so Arui leaned back into the fissure. "Tominae, I'm out! If you can, follow the path! It will lead the way!" She didn't know if the other girl would be able to hear her, or if her voice had been lost to echoes in the dark, or if Tominae was even able to maneuver the passage on her own. A few long quiet moments passed with no sign of the other girl. Arui was preparing to slide back into the passage when she finally heard soft, slow footsteps on damp rock. She saw her friend emerge from the dark a few moments after. She reached out a hand to guide Tominae the rest of the way through and onto the sand where she sank to her knees, exhausted.

Their progress along the wall back towards the Stranger encampment was slow. They were both exhausted after the adventure Arui had conceived, and Tominae was already showing bruises. Halfway between the aperture and the camp, they sat down to rest. It was late afternoon, and the Strangers' washday would be drawing down by now. Arui helped Tominae settle herself more comfortably on the scrub grass that had replaced the sand against the wall, took a few copper pips from the bag leaving the rest concealed with her friend, and disappeared running toward the main city gate. A short time later, she returned, bearing two rough paper cones piled high with white flakes. She handed one to Tominae who inspected it incredulously. "Arui, this isn't--"

"Ices," Arui nodded, grinning. She licked the side of hers and giggled at the sudden chill of frozen water on her tongue, a new experience for them both. The water quickly melted, leaving only the remnant of sugary almond and citron syrup behind. "You almost died today. Eat it before it melts," she said, taking a seat on the scrub next to the other girl. The gray brick wall was warm against her back, but the citron ice was pleasantly cool. Arui and Tominae sat together in silence as they licked at beautifully flavored ice and watched the waves roll in like molten silver. Tominae sighed, and leaned further back into the support of the wall. It was getting late. Their treasure would accomplish so many miracles, ice was only the smallest of them. Good food, clean, strong cloth, medical supplies for Laken and Finia, and sweets for Tominae's siblings from the Invisible Market.

Maybe there would even be enough for a pot of real earth to start a garden.

Before long, they would need to divide the metal pips between them and finish making their way back home. There were watchman patrols to be avoided, explanations to families that would need to be given: about where they had been all day, about the dark marks already drawing themselves under Tominae's skin, and about where the pips had come from. Arui already had answers prepared, but they weren't needed right now. Tominae was here, alive, and so was she. She crunched the last of the blissfully cold flakes between her teeth, settled herself against her friend, and looked out to the sea, feeling free.

Casey Vox

Casey Vox is a queer, nonbinary poet and occasional voice artist. They're also a Concierge of The Rainbow Room (part of The Writers' Rooms), where they moderate discussions on topics of interest to LGBT and ally writers. Casey holds the dubious honor of two-time Vogon Poetry Champion of ICON in Cedar Rapids. Find them on Patreon!

Under-See
Casey Vox

From above, the water blues into the deeps.
The shallows are simpler, safer;
The air is clear.
Letting go that secure footing, to tread
Where toes cannot reach, even *en pointe*,
Well, it certainly *feels* like bravery.
For a while, it is.

In time, the depth becomes comfortable.
The temptation is there -- to remain --
Where the air is, and the light.
There's no need to venture past
The reach of one's grasp.
But there is.

Take a breath.
Deep -- no, deeper --
Stretch your lungs and fill their recesses.
You'll need it, to change the status quo,
To alter your ballast, to
S
I
N
K
Into the depths.

Aquamarine shades to sapphire to...
The ancients, having no word for this blue,
Called the seas wine-dark
And oh, but it is intoxicating.

From below, the light shimmers and scatters.
From below, you can see the tippy-toes of the venturesome.
Down below, you can rest a moment.
But only for a moment.

The need for air strengthens.
Fear creeps in, from the animal brain,
The part that grips the gut and whispers,
Memento mori…
Wait a moment. Face that fear.
This is bravery.

Now rise,
Now breathe,
Now remember.

ALSO CHECK OUT
THE WRITERS' ROOMS

the writers' rooms
www.TheWritersRooms.org

OUR ROOTS

The Writers' Rooms began in late 2015 under the welcoming umbrella of the Iowa Writers' House. We had a simple mission in mind: create a free, accessible community to Iowan writers. The Violet Realm, our sci-fi/fantasy Room, started it all. For two years we incubated under the IWH and learned what our community needed to foster creative minds. It became apparent that if we were going to support our writers, it would be through a community- and crowd-sourced endeavor.

OUR MISSION
Our writing community has the amazing benefit of a massive collection of backgrounds, experiences, and viewpoints. The Writers' Rooms endeavors to bring these wonderful ideas together and help all writers with their craft. We strive to encourage and foster community-based knowledge to help lead literary sessions and provide a safe, positive writing environment. Our Rooms are moderated by both our Concierges and the members of our community. Community-led sessions tap into the wealth of our collective knowledge, allowing our writers to both share their own experiences and learn from other attendees.

The Rooms can't exist without you and your passion and experience!

OUR PEOPLE
Concierge members come from the writing community. All of our current concierges were interested in their topics and became knowledgeable about their genre through reading, writing, and taking lessons of their own. Anyone interested in leading a particular genre- or topic-based Room is welcome to e-mail us at welcome@thewritersrooms.org.

The rest of the Room membership comes from eager writer minds who want to know more about a particular genre or topic. Some have even graciously led lessons for us. We're always looking for more people to share their expertise.

Find out more at: Facebook (IAWritersRooms), and follow us on Instagram (@WritersRooms) and Twitter (@IAWritersRooms).